VENGEA... 35

NA11243LP

VENGEANCE IS SWEET

by
Jerry N. Njoku.

FOP

FOURTH DIMENSION PUBLISHERS

First Published 1985 by

Fourth Dimension Publishing Co., Ltd.
64A City Layout
P. M. B. 1164
Enugu, Nigeria

©1985 by Jerry N. Njoku.

ISBN 978 156 214 5

Cover design by John Oti

Photoset and printed in Taiwan, R.O.C.
BY AI-UNITED INDUSTRIES & SHIPPING INC.
10th Fl., Cheng Chung Great Building
No. 12-1, Lane 5, Lin Shen North Road
Taipei, Taiwan

Dedication

For Philo and Kate

Everyone is talking about crime,
Tell me who are the criminals.

Peter Tosh.

"Who is Obi Ibe?" The school messenger asked, looking up from the piece of paper he held in his hands and with a feeling of importance like one announcing the entrance of the executive president to a state banquet.

All eyes were quickly turned towards Obi's far end seat. Obi jumped his seat as if stung by a serpent. He was filled with fear and surprise. He began to shake with fright. To be summoned to the Principal's office was equivalent to a call for a chat at the police Force Headquarters, Alagbon. One does not often go there. It is always seldom, and when it came, it was for something serious. It was no ideal place for a picnic.

The principal's office had come to be regarded by the students as a place of torture. Obi tried very hard to search his mind for any possible indication for this mid-day summons, but could not bring himself to remember any. This was his second year in the school. He had never been invited to the Principal's office for anything during this period. The only time he saw the principal was on important school occasions or at the morning assemblies which was not often. He was at a loss on what his offénce was. But as far as he knew, he had not done anything bad to invite the principal's wrath. This flushed in a new wave of confidence in him. All these thoughts went through his mind in a flash. "You are wanted by the principal, NOW" the messenger announced, emphasising the 'now' just like the messenger of doom he had came to be regarded as by the students. The whole class looked at Obi with pity and consternation. The aftermath of a visit to the principal's office was what every student dreaded. He was a cane-happy man who derived great satisfaction in donating the cane generously as he would often say, on the bare buttocks of his students, male or female. He believed that the only way to make students learn, behave, and become responsible citizens was through the cane.

He contended that he got to where he was because he was never spared with the rod. His everyday phrase "Spare the rod and spoil the child" was made in prints and conspicuously displayed in all the classrooms.

It was even rumoured among the students, though nobody had had the courage to say it out, that the principal once flogged a member of staff whom he felt behaved like a student. It appeared in the grapevine of the school magazine. Nobody refuted nor accented. Even if the principal called for you to his office in error, you still received the cane for being unfortunate. No one was sure of what amounted to an offence in the face of the principal. He derived great pleasure in watching students wail and beg for mercy. He was a sadist. The prayer therefore on the lips of the students was a constant and stereotyped line "From the fury of the principals cane, good lord deliver us." Obi trailed behind the messenger like a cow being led to the abattoir to be slaughtered "What have you done; Obi what did you do?" the students chorused as they saw him going towards the principal's office. Obi did not answer, rather, he had a vacant and distant look on his face. He had not committed any offence so he could not answer them. Nonetheless, there were doubt and fear written all over his face. Students and masters looked at him with the same thought on their minds as he passed through to the principals office; they would soon hear his wailing.

He was promptly ushered in. To Obi's suprise, he saw his uncle Nwodo seated opposite the principal. He greeted the principal and pretended not to have noticed his uncle.

But still as he looked at his uncle's unsmiling face, he saw grief and sorrow clearly transmitting. Instead of the unfriendly, stern and hostile look that the principal was associated with, it was a kind, subtle and sympathetic expression that Obi saw. The principal looked up from his writing.

"Are you Obi Ibe?"

"Yes Sir."

"Do you know this man?" he asked pointing to Obi's Uncle.

"Yes Sir. He is my father's brother."

"Well, go to the dormitory and pack your things. Your Uncle is waiting to take you home. Take this five naira and safe journey."

Obi stood there transfixed and confused. He looked at his uncle and at the principal, their expressions did not give him any clue. What was the meaning of all these drama. What offence had he committed to entail his outright expulsion from the school? Wouldn't he be given a chance to defend himself before being sent away? He remembered his teacher telling him that one was innocent until proven guilty. He felt this was injustice. He stood still, not moving and not asking questions. He felt his world crumbling under his feet. He started squeezing the five naira in his hand. He wanted to throw the squeezed five naira on the principal's face and damn the consequence but restrained himself. He felt hot blood rush to his face then drained away leaving him cold and shaken. He could not immediately find words. Realizing the hopelessness of his silence, he mustered courage. Looking the principal as he bent writing, asked.

"Excuse me Sir, what have I done Sir?" The principal looked up sharply. This was a question no student dare ask him. His hand quickly picked on his omnipresent cane on the table but dropped it the moment he lifted it. "I said you should go and pack your things and stop staring at me like a moron, and make sure you don't keep your uncle waiting."

Obi still stood there, looking at the principal and his uncle rotatingly. He made no attempt to leave the room. If the principal did not say what his crime was in the presence of his uncle, and if he failed to prove his innocence right before his uncle, he was finished. Nothing that he said at home would be accepted. He was therefore determined to talk to the principal in whatever language at least to prove his innocence. He looked at his uncle who never understood one single word in English and the principal for salvation, but nothing came forth.

He made one last effort to draw the principal's attention from what he was writing.

"But sir .... "

"Don't but me!" the principal snapped at him without raising his head from his writing.

Instead of more effort, Obi looked at his uncle and tears began to roll down his cheeks. His uncle cursed under his breath, all these educated fools. He must have told this boy why he came. They don't have sense.

When the principal raised his head, Obi was still standing there in tears.

"Now you can go." There was no atom of pity or emotion in

his statement. Obi left the office with his uncle following behind him. "What happened?" the students chorused after him. Obi did not answer. He went straight to the dormitory with Ike his friend following like a faithful Alsatian dog.

When Obi got in, he gently packed his few personal effects. What had he? He had a tinker made box containing his housedress, two pairs of trousers and a nylon short he bought from the "Okrika" a name for second hand clothings. Ike helped him with the box and saw them to the gate. Obi stood and looked back at the school. He accepted the box from Ike and his outstretched hands. Still in tears "We shall meet at home," he said, in-between tears. He walked a few steps and turned back again looking at the school building, at the students that sat quietly listening to the teacher's rhetoric, at the hawks hovering over the field in the early morning sun. That would be his last time in the school. He thought. It was a prophesy that came true.

It was a market day. It took them over an hour to get to the motor park. They had to push and squeeze their way through the crowd and with the weight of the box on him it was not easy. When they eventually got to the park, they boarded a bus that had just started to take in passengers. The touts were shouting at the top of their voices to anyone who cared to listen, scrambling and piloting the passengers as if they didn't know their destination. "Umuneke by air, one more chance."

It took the bus just thirty minutes to get filled with passengers. Within this interval, Obi tried hard to think about what was responsible for this home going. Definitely, since he was sure he had not committed any offence in school, and his uncle had come for him, something must have happened. What was it? He smelt something ominous but could not decipher his thoughts in concrete terms. Was any of his parents dead? He closed his eyes at the thought. What an unhealthy thinking he said to himself.

Two hours later, they arrived in the village square. Everyone looked at him with the same eyes that the students had looked him earlier in the day. It was with pity and concern. Just then, he heard wailings of women and children towards the direction of their compound. That confirmed the obvious. Those shouting and wailings were always synonymous with death. Who could it be? His father or mother? He love and respected them both and did not want to loose any at this stage of his life.

For the first time since his uncle came for him, he talked. "Dede Nwodo, what happened? Why are people crying?"

"You will see for yourself when you get home." He replied stonely. As their compound came into view, he saw palmfronds sheds. Some people were seated mournfully, some were drinking palmwine from a big calabash while others were struggling at the oilbeen cake placed on the table in the centre. A bottle of 'Akamere' the local gin, was there untouched.

When Obi entered the compound through the outhouse called "Ovu", new waves of tears erupted volcanically. Obi saw his mother in between four other women. They were trying to pin her down in her effort to rush towards Obi. Her eyes were red and swollen with tears. Obi dropped his box and ran towards her.

"Mama, Mama!"

"Your father is dead, my son." She said stretching out her hands as if begging death to take her along.

"We don't have anybody again. My enemies are now happy. They have done their wish. Your father did not die his natural death, my son."

Obi threw himself to the ground and started wriggling in tears. Uche, his brother who had just turned three years ran to him there.

Dede! Dede! They say papa has died and nobody to bring me rats and rabbits anymore. Will you bring for me?"

Strong hands immediately seized Obi. "Look son," said Echendu, his maternal Uncle. "I know you are still a child, but no matter how small a son is, he has his father's palmwine on Orie day. Come and see your father's corpse before you start behaving like a woman." Obi followed him obediently.

"Remember," he continued "Nobody cries in the presence of a dead person, else the person cries also."

That trick worked. Obi stopped crying instantly. He was led to an ante-room. There, he met his uncles and aunt and some elders from the village. They all sat or stood round the corpse like in a religious ritual. That was Obi's first time of seeing a corpse. He had just turned thirteen but was too big for his age. He exhibited such a calm. The nostrils of the dead man were blocked with cotton wool. Despite that, his father laid as if asleep. He stared hard at the body, covered, lying on top of the bamboo bed. Remembering it was his father and that he will never wake up or talk to him again, he wanted to cry, but remembering again Uncle Echendu's warning, he stopped himself before the first drop of tears could escape. Much as he knew, he still wanted very much to stay alive.

"Okay, take the boy out," said Obinna, the oldest man in the Village.

Obi was again led out. By now, his playmates had heard the news of his arrival. They gathered round him.

"Sorry Obi," they all said together. Obi was at a lost what to do, at least not at his present age. He had not been in such a predicament before. Things went too fast for Obi's understanding and comprehension. Fowls were killed, goats slaughtered, foo-foo were pounded in several mortars as if it were a feast day.

Palmwine arrived in big calabashes. Obi just sat at a quiet corner with his mother watching the goings. People looked at him in utter amazement and open-mouthed bewilderment, at the type of calm he kept. Was it that the fact had not hit him or was it self composure? They wondered at his equanimity. It came to Obi suddenly that evil was perhaps always more impressive and much better than good. He was sold on the childish thinking that God takes away the good and innocent and allows the evil more time on earth necessary for repentance. He suddenly became oblivious of his surroundings. Pictures of hardship and suffering conjured up in his mind.

He was recalled from this unpleasant thought by a sudden sound of explosion from cannon fired outside. Gbam! Gbam! like in a battle field. It continued. Obi counted along as it sounded. At the end of the fifteenth shot, shouts rented the air. The native drummers took it up. It was like lightning after thunder.

It roused the people to absolute frenzy. Matchets were brandished and clattered in mid-air. The rhythm of the drumming increased in tempo, recounting the heroic deeds of Ibe, Obi's father. People danced mechanically. Everyone was dancing and making merry. Some were getting drunk.

That night, in a quiet corner, obi sized up the whole situation. He was shocked at the prevalence of such merry making at the instant of death. Death had come to mean nothing to friends and neighbours. Only the affected feels the pangs of sorrow. If not so, he saw no reason why Ekenna, a member of the clan and in fact his fathers friend and age-mate, with a common bond, fought for a piece of goat meat he claimed was denied him and even later got drunk, fighting almost everyone present, nor could he comprehend why his father's age group members refused to touch anything or take part in the burial ceremony until they were given a pot of wine, two tubers of yam, a fowl and a bottle of Schnapps Aromatic Gin, not even the local 'Akamere' that was handy.

People fought freely and unashamedly over food and drink. It was an eye-sore and quite unbecoming. Infact it was a bizarre spectacle. People were either demanding for more palmwine like in a marriage feast or for yam as if it was just after harvest. Some went into the barn on their own accord if refused. It looked more of looting. The sympathies were false, it never went deep. Nobody cared for what would become of the family of the dead after the burial ceremony. Death was fast becoming another social gathering for eating, drinking, dancing and making merry. Things became worst if it was a man of means. It was fast developing into a cult.

Obi was sick of the whole environment. It was stinking with hypocrisy and equally repulsive. The debris of the values of the society were fast corroding and falling into oblivion. The society was fast changing negatively. Things were no more what they used to be. Some would just cry into the compound and seconds later would settle for either a cup or two of palmwine or would be seen dismantling a plate of pounded yam or foofoo. The young ones were not left out. They were seen making passes at the girls! The more successful ones went out with the girls into the dark night defiling the stillness of the night. Those who remained behind danced in pairs as if in a party. Infact it had became a party.

The most sorrowful moment was when Obi was asked to come and shovel in the first sand on the coffin after it was laid in the grave. He was the eldest son of the deceased and custom demanded it of him, his age notwithstanding. This show attracted public sympathy for Obi.

The death of Obi's father left a hollow both in the purse and in the daily life of the family. The barn was raided by the mourners. They left almost nothing. Only two goats remained in the goat shed. Four went with the burial. The chickens were all gone, more were even bought to meet the demands. The whole compound became very lonely. Obi was the only grown up apart from the mother. Noises re-echoed. The noise made by rats were greatly magnified. They all sounded like approaching feet.

The heads of all members of the family were clean shaven and shone like newly made clay pots. Most of the masculine jobs were done by Obi with occasional help drifting in from his maternal home. Adaku did the house work. His mother was not to do anything for sometime, not even cooking her food. Custom demanded that she be fed differently from other members of the family at least for sometime.

Life drabbed on routinely like this for a month. The sympathizers were thinning down. Some were still looking forward to be entertained. Such was the custom. A pot of palmwine was provided daily for this purpose by Nwodo. But this never lasted long, it lasted just for a month. It stopped automatically when Obi was sent by his mother to Uncle Nwodo for money for the family to buy food at the famous Nkwo market. Nwodo leashed out venom and poured curses on Obi and his mother. When he came back with the news, his mother broke into fresh tears in recapitulation.

From then onwards, Obi began seeing himself in a different light. His life seemed to be changing. Obi still burned with the desire to go back to school. When the new term was about to re-open, Obi told his mother of his inmost wish to go and join his mates. He had not lost much time at home.

The decision on such delicate issues as in this, more so when, it involved money rests on the father of the house. So on his mother's advise, Obi decided to talk to his Uncle.

At first, it was difficult for him. He had never stood in the presence of this Uncle to utter a word. But realizing his predicament, he summoned courage. It was the third day after talking to his mother that the opening came.

After lunch that afternoon, Obi went to his Uncle's house. He has just finished a meal of pounded cassava when Obi got in, the plates still on the table. Obi took the plates to the Kitchen. By the time he came back, his Uncle had dozed off. The pounded cassava was indeed a local sleeping tablet. Not knowing what to do, go back home and come again, wake him up, he decided to shuffle his legs on the floor. His Uncle stirred and opened his eyes. Obi sat opposite him confused, not knowing how to go about it when his uncle began dozing again.

"Dede," Obi called at him.

"Yes, what is that?"

"Dede, you know the school will re-open next week, I have come to see you about it."

"See me about what?" he snapped at him fully awake now.

"About the re-opening of the school."

"Let the school re-open, and what has the re-opening got to do with me?"

"I would like to go back to school and complete my education."

"EH!" he said sarcastically, "go back and complete your education, and who is withholding you from going back, or are the masquerades on the road?"

"Dede, but that is not what I mean, I need to buy the things to take to school. Tomorrow is Ahia Nkwo and its going to be the last before we resume. Things are cheaper there."

"Look my son, you are wasting my time. Have I asked you not to go to Ahia Nkwo to buy whatever you need to go to school with? Why bother me? Ehe! Go to the market, buy the whole market if you like. I want to go for my tapping. Look at the sky, it is threatening to rain."

Nwodo made an effort to leave. Obi rubbed his hands together in exasperation at what his Uncle said. At the death of his father, all that he had passed to his brother Nwodo. He had already started tapping the palms that belonged to his father. He was sure his Uncle understood what he meant and the role he would play but was deliberately shying away from the responsibility. He therefore, decided to hit the nail no the head.

"Dede," he resumed. "All I want from you is the money to buy the things."

"Money for what?" he shouted at Obi. "Did you give me any money to keep for you? Or did your father told you he gave me money for your College to hold in trust for you?"

"But Dede----------"

"But what? Oho! Your mother sent you to come and meet me, bad woman. When she was busy eating up all the things her husband had, she never remembered that her son would go to College. If she wants you to go to College, let her go to her kinsmen. They would not be doing much for their sister if they send you to College."

"By the way," he continued. "Do you still think you would grow more than this? Your father had just died. His yams are all on the farm, the palms require cutting, your small brothers and sisters will eat, all these need your attention, and you are talking of going back to College. College my foot! I am sure it is your mother that is putting these foolish ideas into your head. No wonder! I said it when my brother wanted to marry her. Instead of you staying at home and becoming useful to yourself, you want to go and waste your time and money. Well! not my own money, not the money Nwodo suffered to get."

"Besides, one who goes to the house of frog and ask for a seat, does he see anyone occupied by frog, his host?"

Obi immediately realized that what all those talks amounted to was that he would not have a hand in his education, since none of his own children had attained such height. He knew that it was his father's earnest wish before his death to see him at least through the grammar school. The rhythm and tempo in the beating of his life's drumming was changing, all what it entailed was to change his steps also in line with the new beating. Nevertheless, he was disappointed. Uncertainty now loomed ahead of him. He now realized that the death of his father has started to destroy the edifice of his hopes.

Obi soon settled in his new role. He learnt fast how to tend to the yam tendrils, stake them, climbing of plam trees for the oil and kernel and various other odd jobs. With some help coming in from here and there, Obi was able to provide the much needed three square meals for the family. Yet he was not satisfied. He felt that nature had denied him something, something very important to him, a secondary education. His saddest moments were when the students came home on holidays or attended the towns student union meetings at the village square or the extra-mural vacation classes, or when with their towels hung over their necks dallying over cleaning either the village hall or the church, it was worst when they prepare to go back to school. Inside him, he still burned with the desire for that formal education, acquire the societal tag to be called a student. He however never mentioned it again to his mother. He remember the last time he mentioned it, his mother had immediately gone in and started crying. It brought memories of her late husband flashing back to her. Obi's only consolation rested on the poor man's phrase "Once there is life, there is hope."

Six months after his father's death, it seemed that his destiny was to change for the better. He was offered to be taken to Aba by one of the sons of the clan who came home and saw him doing nothing concrete.

The thought of leaving the village for Aba put Obi in high spirits. Though Aba was just sixty kilometres away from home, but there was still that difference between his peer group who had left immediately after their primary school and those who remained behind in the village. They always came home on festivals with new shoes and baggy trousers and more money to spend. Those at home always look inferior to them. They were not always free to mix with them.

Obi had never been to a big city before, he was therefore exhilarated. The only tarred road he had seen was the one that ran through their school. He burned with the desire to see what people called city-life.

Amadi Okonkwo, known for his generosity and good-nature in the village had volunteered to take Obi to Aba to stay with him and if possible learn a trade of his choice. He did not want to impose on Obi his own trade - Tailoring, though it will be cheaper for him to see Obi through.

Amadi was among those who never forgot favours done to him. He owed Obi's father a favour before his death. Since he could not pay him now, he intended to manifest it on his children and on Obi since he was the only grown up in the family, and at such a time when the help was needed.

It all happened during his apprenticeship as a tailor. He had been driven home by his master for tools he lost. In actual fact, he did not lose the tools, it was an unknown apprentice who took it. The rule then was that, tools were entrusted to a particular apprentice on each working day. Any tool lost during your day was your responsibility and should be replaced by you. There was no compromise.

When he got home for the money, much as he expected, there was no money to buy the missing tools. A land was proposed to be pledged to raise money, but it could not make up for the amount. His parents therefore went to the village shylock, Uzo Dimgba. Uzo was known for his unscrupulousness and cheating. He could milk a man dry. He demanded a hundred percent interest on the ten pounds to be borrowed, and two hundred percent if the money was not paid back in six months. Amadi's parents agreed, but Uzo went further to demand for two fowls, a jar of wine and six tubers of yams as token before he could give the money out.

The news of Uzo Dimgba's extortion was not new to people in the village but this particular one to a kinsman angered Ibe, Obi's father. With anger boiling in him, he ran to Uzo Dimgba's house and confronted him with the story.

"Dimgba," he stammered. "Did Okonkwo Adibe come to you for money?"

"Yes, and what is your business in that?"

"My business?"

"Yes! I mean your business! If he comes to me for money, so what?"

"Remember that a one legged fowl is never sold to a Kinsman?"

"He comes to me as a customer and because I have the money. If he is not satisfied with my conditions, he can go elsewhere. Or if you are not satisfied with that either, you can give him your own money free.''

"You have no shame, you can sell your mother for money," he blurted out.

"Look, Ibe, if you intend to put your fingers into my eyes in this village, you will live to regret it. Mind your own business and I will mind mine. Remember that if a child throws his father up, his loin cloth will surely cover his face.''

"You are not going to milk Okonkwo. He was my elder brother's friend and I am not going to sit and close my eyes while you cheat him. You are a big cheat.''

With this, he bolted out and made straight to Okonkwo's house. Nobody was in when he got there, except for some kids playing outside the "ovu". He left a message for Okonkwo to see him as soon as he came back. Even the children read the urgency in his voice.

When Okonkwo got home, his son shouted at him in exasperation at not going to Dimgba's house. The last day for him to return was the next day. Okonkwo willingly apologized. It was then a child told him of Ibe's message. Okonkwo asked his son to get the things ready and that they would go as soon as he came back. Ibe was not a man to be kept waiting.

Ibe was sitting in his Ovu, brooding over a calabash of palmwine and the hurricane lamp burning when he saw the silhouette of an approaching figure. He quickly adjusted his loin cloth.

"Mman Mman!" Okonkwo greeted as he came in.

"Please take your seat. How are the children?"

"Fine! I heard -------"

"Wait first, let us break the kola." He stood up and dipped his hand into a goat skin bag that hung overhead. His hand emerged with a kolanut and a drinking gourd.

"Kola has come."

"I have not seen it until I hear the sound in my mouth," Okonkwo added humourously.

Ibe broke the kola into two and handed one over to him. He gave it a bite.

"Ehe! I have seen the kola." He took the drinking gourd and poured himself wine from the calabash.

"Is this a fresh palm or overnight?" He asked as he sipped the palm and raised up his head.

"It is overnight. You know I don't take the fresh wine."

"That is what I tell these small boys who just go spoiling the palm, who don't know the difference between the front and back. Who would believe that this is an overnight wine?"

Ibe was flattered but allowed it to hang.

"Eh! Nnayi Okonkwo, I sent for you. I heard you went to Dimgba for money."

"Yes my brother. It is all these children and problems. When an old man like me could have been looking after my wife and myself, I am still slaving for children."

"Well, they are our responsibility. We brought them into the world. Even if they become Kings tomorrow, they must still come to us, at least for advice. But that is by the way. I heard the condition Dimgba gave. One thing I still remembered was your relationship with Nwaogwugwu, my elder brother before he died. How much do you want?"

"Eh! Please my brother, come again, I don't seem to get what you mean."

"I said how much did you ask Dimgba to lend you?"

"My brother, it is ten pounds."

"Wait for me, I am coming." Ibe went into the compound and emerged three minutes later with ten pounds five shillings. Then he counted the money in the presence of Okonkwo.

"This is the ten pounds. Whenever you get it, you return it back to me. I don't ask for any interest. Give your son this five shillings for his transport. Nobody can ever tell tomorrow. Time might come when he will help my own children."

Okonkwo was lost of words to say, he dumbly accepted the money. It was difficult to believe this magnanimity. Dimgba had offered to give at a hundred percent and fowls, yams. He had agreed, and here is a man whom not only refused interest, but from whom he had never sought help from.

"My brother, thank you for this, I don't know what to say or how to thank you. I only pray that the spirits of our father keep you to reap the fruits of the good things you do in this village."

"What is the need of being Kinsmen if we cannot help one another in time of need?" said Ibe.

They had more drinks before Okonkwo left. Back at home, his son Amadi was fuming with anger when his father walked in.

"Papa where have you been all the time. Is it Ibe's house alone?"

Okonkwo ignored his question.

"Please call me your mother and come along with her."

When his wife and son came in, he undid his loin cloth and placed the ten pounds five shillings on the table.

"Amadi, count that money first."

"It is ten pounds five shillings. Where did you get this from?" asked the anxious wife and son.

"I am coming to that. Look, Amadi, don't underestimate any man. Not all those that make noise have something to back up the noise. I used to tell you people that not all people that call father will go to heaven."

"Most of you who reel in the church are not better than we that give respect to our ancestors."

"Answer our questions," chorused both mother and son.

"Ibe called me and this is what I came back with. No interest. No yams no fowls.

"God will surely reward him." said Okonkwo's wife "Why don't we take the fowls and yams to him?"

Quickly, Amadi carried the wrapped yams and the fowl to Ibe's house. Further surprise awaited them. Ibe not only rejected the gift, but added six more tubers for Amadi.

Six months later, Amadi with his parents returned the ten pounds with an addition of five pounds, impressing on him to accept it as a token for their gratitude. Ibe only counted out his ten pounds and returned the five pounds back.

"You will need the money to buy tools for your son," he had said. As for the palmwine they brought, in his words, he contended that "If palmwine comes for good or bad, we shall drink it. Wine that comes to the house is never returned." That was twenty years ago. A strong family tie had developed from there.

When he got home and saw Obi idle, he saw it as an opportunity to pay back the good turn by his father. Obi's mother accepted. Though she knew what Obi meant to the family now, she was ready to sacrifice anything for a brighter future for his son.

Obi left the village after the planting season. He had helped his mother plant cassava, cocoyam and attended to the yam tendrils, putting all supporting sticks. Since Aba was just two naira fare home, it was agreed that Obi should be coming home every month end to help her mother in as much as it will not interrupt his work.

When Obi arrived at Aba, he was given a red or better called a white carpet reception. Oriaku, Amadi's wife gave him water for his bath. Food was served to Obi on the huge dining table. Obi ate silently. He was lost in Sir Arthur Conan Doyle's "LOST WORLD". Would life continue to be like this for him? What a nice woman. He has heard of her but was meeting her for the first time. Is she not from the Okagbue's family? Then, she must be an exception. The Okagbue's that dreaded his family.

This treatment was not to last long. The families of Oriaku's parents, the Okagbue's had never been in the best of terms with Obi's family. They had been in a land dispute where charm was openly used. In the end, Obi's family won. An unspoken enmity developed. They never crossed ways.

Obi's mother was initially opposed to Obi's going on that grounds, but being a devout Christian, and thinking that the passage of time must have eroded whatever ill-feelings that might have been created at least in the minds of the young ones and for the fact that neither Obi nor his father were directly involved. Infact it was between Obi's grandfather and Oriaku's. She felt that now that Oriaku had been married into another family and a Christian fanatic, things were bound to change. Little did she know that the family blood ran through all the Okagbue's.

Oriaku did not show any open resentment when his husband brought Obi from home. She pretended in the presence of her husband that she was happy over it. But deep down in her mind she was not happy. Her family dreaded anybody from Obi's family like a plague. The school teacher was even bribed so that nobody from either family sat together. The children were not allowed to play together. When both families embraced Christianity, things did not improve either, they never sat together on the same bench in the church. If perchance one turns and sees that the person direct-ly behind him was from either family, she or he immediately chang-ed seat. Obi's mother was the only exception.

Within a week, Oriaku, despite her professed Christianity, started to show her family trait. Obi did all the menial jobs. He washed the kids, washed their plates even though Adaku, her eldest daughter was thirteen. Obi never ate until her children finished eating them, soup will be added to the remains of what the children left for Obi to eat with. Oriaku constantly reminded him that it was not her who killed his father but his wickedness that killed him.

To Obi's suprise, during the night prayers which was a matter of routine, Oriaku prayed, shook, speaking in tongues as if possess-ed by the Holy Spirit. She will pray for hours calling on the God and his son the Lord Jesus Christ to come and save this world of sin and to save the sinners. She would always end up with "Surely the wicked shall inherit enternal hell fire, Amen."

Obi always like to catch her gaze after such praying sessions but she would deliberately avoid him. All this gave Obi food for thought. Considering the type of treatment metted out to him by this woman. He was at a lost what heaven meant. If such women will have a place in heaven, Okeke the priest of 'Ajala' or the 'Ogbalogu' priest of Umuevule must also be there; theirs was no hypocrisy. He thought on this new breed of preachers who go about the villages defiling the girls popularly called the daughters of Mary (Umungberi) and some Christian mothers who dare submit themselves to them, thinking that making love with a man of God was a passport to heaven. The brand of preachers who preach "Do what I say and not what I do." He felt that preachers and those who claimed to be born again christians should give a good exam-ple and testimony of their faith. By so doing, more were prone to be converted.

Nevertheless, this did not make Obi lose faith in his own God. He wanted to tell the woman outright at the end of evening prayer that she was a hypocrite, but courage failed him.

Two months after Obi arrived in Aba, the evil pursuing him

struck again. Amadi Okonkwo had a fatal accident on his motorcycle while returning from his shop one Monday night. He was hospitalized. This lasted for three months. These three months were the most gruelsome in Obi's life. His feeding was initially reduced to twice daily with the pretext that the breadwinner was not in. All sort of inhuman treatment was meted out to Obi. He was even made to wash Oriaku's bloodstained pants she used for her menstrual period. This Obi did without minding.

Early in the morning, Obi would be sent out to hawk bread and will be given ten kobo for breakfast. Obi roamed the streets of Aba with a tray full of bread on his head and absolutely nothing in his stomach. If he came back early, he received the cane for coming home early and if he came back late, it was worst. He will be accused for shirking his responsibilities at home. Such was the life he led. Most often, his school mates who were now second year or third year apprentices in their various trades saw him. They pitied him and often gave him money from the tips they got from impressed customers. This money when seen by Oriaku was always a cause of sorrow for Obi. He would be beaten, called names and again reminded that his mother was languishing in hunger at home.

His friends advised him to leave the woman to stay with them. This Obi refused. He felt it was ingratitude to leave at a time when the man who brought him was still lying in hospital. If he was to leave and which he was determined to do, it would be after Amadi must have been discharged from the hospital.

Two months after Amadi was discharged from hospital and when he was fully back to his trade, Obi told him of his intention to leave for home. He thanked Amadi for his generosity, kindness and concern but regretted that it was better for him to stay at home and if he wanted to learn any trade, it would be somewhere nearer home, because of late, his mother had started to be sickly due to over labour. He contended that all the world was worth nothing to him without his mother. But the main reason for wanting to leave, he did not tell him.

Amadi was moved by the boys speech. He explained his conditions to Obi. Nevertheless, he gave Obi a hundred naira to try his hands on anything he liked.

At the sight of the hundred naira, Oriaku's eyes shone with hatred. But she dare not challenge the decision of her husband. In her hypocritical way, she expressed her disappointment at Obi's leaving just at a time when they were about fixing him up somewhere, she said that she was sure they will actually miss his company particularly the children that had grown to be used to him.

As Obi boarded a bus home he reflected on his stay at Aba, and concluded that if going to a town meant this, he was contented with staying at home and doing whatever God provided for him. He felt that if not for Oriaku, he would have enjoyed his stay there. He vowed never to stay or go out again with a married man. Most times, the man goes off to work and does not know what happens at home. The treatment given to you while he was around was a direct opposite of the one you will be subjected to when he is out. You dare not report such treatment, else you may be accused of trying to destabilise the entire family. As for the one hundred naira, Obi did not know what to do with it. His mother will decide.

When Obi got home, his mother rushed out to welcome him. Streaks of tears ran through her cheeks. Obi looked spent up. He was lean as if just recovered from a malaria attack.

"Nna," she called his pet name.

"Mama."

"What is wrong with you? Were you sick?"

"No, mama."

Quickly, she led him in and prepared hot water for him. Food was immediately brought. Obi finished the whole bowl with his mother watching.

"Hm I now know you have not been fed well. I think I have always been saying it that not all those township people feed well. In the morning they give people this sheep urine called tea and they call it food. In the afternoon they measure gari.

"Thank God you are back my son. How did that woman treat you?"

"Mama, wait until I have rested."

That night, Obi unfolded what he saw since he went to Aba. He exonerated Amadi who was always away to the shop not to come back until it was night. When he showed her the money, she opened her mouth in surprise.

Things went on uneventful for a whole calendar year. Though Obi was fifteen, he was fully grown. During the Christmas celebrations of the second year, Obi travelled to his maternal home to see his grandmother as was the yearly practice. His cousin Paul was at home on his annual leave which coincided with the Christmas and New Year. Obi had a lengthy discussion with him. In the end, he offered to take Obi to Lagos where numerous opportunities abound, where Obi could be working and at the same time be attending evening classes. That created an opening and he was quick to make use of it. He saw it as an opportunity to accomplish his obsession.

His mother quickly consented when she was told. For the first time, her face shone with relief and happiness. She had been very much concerned about Obi's future. Now, God had answered her prayers and sent a benevolent spirit to their rescue.

Arrangements were quickly made about Obi's departure. Two days after the New Year celebration, Obi found himself in a Lagos bound luxurious bus. His joy knew no bounds. He asked scores of questions as the vehicle tore its way towards the capital city. His cousin laughed at his excitement. It was reminiscence of his own first visit to Lagos. It was always so with anyone visiting Lagos for the first time. He knew that such excitement will not last long when one faces the grim reality of Lagos life, it fades away by itself.

Obi's image of Lagos was greatly exaggerated. He pictured Lagos to be a land flowing with opportunities, a place where only little effort was required for the attainment of one's desires; where everyone lived in luxury as reflected by the people who came home yearly for either the Christmas or New Year celebrations or both. They were always seen gorgeously dressed and had the cash to split about. This had accounted for the immensity of his joy at the prospect of going to Lagos. Little did he know that those people lived for those celebrations. All yearly savings were spent on such occasions for them to begin again. It was a circular living.

The lights of Lagos at night, like a million glittering stars as they entered the outskirts of the city, made him squeal with delight. Now that he was in Lagos, he was going to have and enjoy all the much talked about excitements and frivolities it offered. But as they boarded a bus to Bariga, where people lived in makeshift houses just for shelter, where the stinking smell of obstructed drainage blended with the air to give a very disagreeable smell; where nightsoil men had become lords and a constant menace with their loaded buckets of human excretion; where the slightest provocation would make them deposit it along the street to the discomfort of the people around; where hurricane lamps peeped from cracks in walls of the houses; He felt disappointed. His hopes began to falter. His daydreams began to subside. Was this the Lagos? He seemed to ask.

As they walked from the bus-stop towards Paul's house, Obi began to look at the world in its true perspective. Things don't always appear the way they are painted. Most stories might appear impressive in the minds of the author just for a particular purpose and for a particular audience. The picture of Lagos he was now seeing was in direct and sharp contrast with what he was made to believe. He had only expected to see skyscraper or at least storeyed buildings and few bungalows all over, with electricity and planned tarred roads with fountains of water everywhere as portrayed in most of the postcards he saw sent by people from Lagos to brothers and sisters as home, but he failed to realize that places fare not just like their pictured postcards.

More disappointment awaited him as they got to Paul's house. Paul lived in what could be rightly called a Kitchen but was converted into a living room because of acute accommodation shortage. The room was just enough to contain an eight springed bed, a multi-purpose cupboard; which served as food store and a table and two chairs, which cracked under a ten year-old weight. Every other thing was pushed under the bed for lack of space. The little passage left was not even spacious enough for the two of them to stand akimbo at the same time. There appeared to be an unbalanced force between the smoke coming in from the makeshift kitchen next door and the constant humming of the fan as it sent out its

22

mechanized air. Obi looked into the room with scrutiny but did not say anything. His cousin read it all on his face. He reserved all comments and explanations. Now that Obi was in Lagos, he would allow him to discover what Lagos was himself.

Nevertheless, his first month in Lagos was no doubt exciting. His cousin made everything possible to make him feel at home. He was given a warm reception. On weekends, he was taken to places of interest and exotic spots of the city.

Obi did not know which to admire, the snake-like Eko bridge, the flyovers, the unceasing flow of traffic with its various brands of cars as he had never dreamt existed, the assorted types of wares exhibited at window shops or the towering building that appeared to him ready to fall as he walked passed it. He looked agape. His cousin would walk yards ahead talking to himself, believing Obi to be behind him. Waiting for a response, he would just turn to see Obi standing afar, looking like a moron at either the people, cars or wares with mouth wide open.

As time progressed, he was gradually introduced to the swinging night life of Lagos. He saw with surprise, girls young enough to still be under the care of their parents clinging to men and openly making love to them unabashed at odd hours of the night in various corners of the clubs. His moral upbringing came into direct conflict with this large scale immorality that seemed to transcend the society. Everywhere he went to was just the same.

At the end of the second month, with the help of his cousin, he had written more than twenty applications to various establishments, either as an office boy, office cleaner or factory hand. None was acknowledged, there were no invitations for interview.

Towards the end of the third month, his cousin came home one evening with the news that a place was open in their Factory as a labourer. Obi was very happy. It surged into him new hopes. He was cheered up. But when his cousin mentioned the string attached, he was sad. The job was to be offered at a kola.

"Eh! and I forgot while coming. The kolanut tree in our barn would have even served the whole lot of people in your Company. Anyway, I am sure they sell kola around here. By the way, how many kolanuts would he be able to finish?"

Paul burst into laughter, nearly laughing himself into convulsions. Tears streaked from his eyes as he laughed and rolled on the bed. Obi did not understand why his cousin laughed. What had he said that demanded such outburst of laughter?

Kolanuts? Well, if a man needed just kolanuts to help him get a job, why not give him as many as he liked. When Paul stopped, Obi looked up to him for an explanation.

"Obi, you don't seem to understand. This kolanut is not what it appears to mean. This kolanut means money, and he is demanding fifty naira as his kolanut."

"Fifty naira?" Obi said surprised.

"Yes! fifty naira."

"Must we offer money to the company before I am employed?" asked Obi, not yet in the picture.

"Obi, this is Lagos where you get what you want with what you have. You are not in the village. You don't expect things to be so easy. This kola is not meant for the company but the "Oga" who is responsible for employment. Without the money, there will be no employment for you, and unfortunately, he had given me only this week, failing which, chance will be given to another person who is more serious."

"But where do I get fifty Naira from?"

"You will please lend me fifty naira to pay if you are sure I would get the job. If I get started, I will repay you."

"Obi, you have just landed. You are a J.J.C. (Johnny Just Come). You don't understand Lagos. I have been in Lagos for three years now and life has not been easy. Consider all those outings we have had, our feeding, my transportation, clothing, constant demand from people at home and other unorthodox way a youngman spends money. How can I save on a salary of a hundred and twenty-five naira or a hundred and fifty if I don't work overtime? I pay twenty naira for this bed-sitter called a room. So my dear, I don't have fifty naira anywhere to bring. If I had, I should not have mentioned it to you. Lagos is no man's land. It is not as easy as you think. Many have thought like you before, many have come and gone but Lagos still remains the same.''

Obi could not buy Paul's story. He still wondered why anybody on such a fantastic salary compared with people at home could not make a saving of at least fifty naira monthly. If he got employed, he hoped to save a hundred naira monthly, he thought.

"Okay, what do we do now. The question is I don't know anyone, where do I get the money from?''

"Since you have registered in the Town Union as an applicant, and luckily tomorrow is the monthly meeting, you will ask for a loan of sixty-naira to pay for a job. They all will understand. They have all done so before. You will promise to pay back at the end of the third month after you get started.''

"Em! are you sure? Will I get it?'' he asked, excitement mounting in him.

"There is no doubt about that. It has been a standing practice. By that, they feel they are helping you stand on your feet. Also, they feel since the money belonged to the meeting, in the event of non-payment, the loss was shared out among all.'' "The point is, no one would say no even though he hates your guts. No one would like to be named as the person who prevented you from getting a job. They are all afraid of dipping their hands into their pocket to give you the money.''

"Think what story that would make at home, tongues would surely wag against such person. He would be seen as the hawk that has perched and refused the eagle to perch. What other alternative then than to give out the money from a common purse.''

"But wouldn't it be treacherous for one to collect the money and refuse to pay.''

"Obi, that is Lagos and what it stands for. In the village, most people are sincere and honest, they are very conscious of what the public says about them. Consider a situation where you pay the kola and failed to get the job.''

"I will demand for my money and where he refuses, I will call in the elders.'' As if not quite sure of what he had just said, "Or are there no elders in this place?''

"My brother, you make a mistake. Lagos is a conglomeration

of tribes with different ethnic norms and values. You are your 'elder', I am my 'elder'. We are all here to make a living.''

"Then I will report to the police.''

"Again brother, you make a mistake. The money you gave was a bribe, and remember, it is a crime to offer bribe. No receipts are made for bribes. It is entirely at your own risk. Besides, you will be making more money for the police. What the man has to do is to give part of the money to them and they will also expect you to grease their palms for performing their duty. On the long run, you will be left the worse.''

Doubt filled Obi's mind on this morbid revelation. He had thought that everywhere was home with a simple society where justice was not denied, though pursued in a crude manner. Was he to get the loan and accept the risk involved? He was confused. If things failed, who would pay back the money, Paul or himself?

Paul instantly read his thought.

"Obi, I know what you are thinking about. I know what your fears are. You will definitely get the job, just let us get the money first. I know him very well.''

"That is alright.'' Nevertheless, he did not sound very convinced.

That night, Obi dreamt sweet and promising dreams. Dreams of himself in the factory working to earn money. He dreamt of his mother, brothers and sisters whom he had not seen since he got to Lagos, all clad in nice clothings as gift from their son in Lagos.

He was awakened the following morning by the clattering bell of the vendor. Paul never missed the Sunday Times. When he came back from church that morning, he picked up his pen to write a letter to his mother, breaking the news. But when he started with "Dear Mother'', he was at a loss on what to write. It would be better to wait until he got the job. The news would be more meaningful, he thought.

The early rise in the mornings for work, the struggle to board a bus and his new job gave Obi a novel experience. He enjoyed and liked every bit of it. His first day at work gave him the same experience he had on his first day in the Grammar School. It was an exciting experience. Everybody was answered with "Yes Sir" even the messengers. He never seemed to be tired for eight hours. He was very humble in performing any piece of work given to him as if it would attract more pay. The old hands just looked and laughed at him. They knew Obi would soon relax after a month or two. They all did the same.

By the end of the month, Obi had worked overtime to the tune of fifty naira. When he got his pay packet, he carefully extracted the money and counted. It was one hundred and seventy naira. He could not believe his eyes. As he walked to the bus-stop, he kept looking over his shoulders for any likely attack on him. This was the first time he had owned a sum of money as big as that. He was ready to protect it at all cost. Inside the bus, he firmly held his side pocket and was constantly looking at the lady who sat next to him. The lady must have thought it was all in admiration and she reciprocally smiled at Obi who never responded.

When Obi got home, he locked himself up and carefully spread the money on the bed. He just sprang up and took a dive for the bed, as if for the swimming pool. He laid on the money with a childish fantasy. Before his cousin came home two hours later, Obi had counted the money the tenth time. Even when he heard a knock, he quickly took a dive for the money and ducked it under the mattress before opening the door even though he knew it was his cousin.

That night, Paul advised him to open up an account to save some and send money home. He refused to accept money from him for their joint feeding except for the few times they went out together. He promised to give him three months of grace during which Obi must have settled the loan and rehabilitate his mother and brothers and sisters.

Exactly at the end of the second month, Paul was transfered to Kano. Obi was seriously affected. He had lived to respect his cousin who was the only person in the chain of the extended family who had as much cared for his future and welfare. Besides, he was just trying to find his feet in the swinging city of Lagos. When the Kano-bound train left, he stood in tears looking at the train as Paul waved him bye-bye.

Within two months of taking care of himself, pay for the rent, transport himself to work, feed himself and send money home, he started to discover the difference between reality and ideal. He saw what Paul meant when he called him J.J.C. He started to see Lagos as an intricate and complex society. Gradually his monthly visit to the bank to deposit part of his salary reduced. Instead, he went to withdraw.

After enrolling for evening classes he was hardly able to feed himself and still pay the school fees of his brothers that he had instructed to go back. Nevertheless, he persevered. He worked overtime on weekends to enable him to make both ends meet. He was burdened with great responsibilities. He wanted to live to the sugary promises he made to his mother. Inspite of all this, Obi made progress. At least, everybody in the family up to school age was in school.

Three years later, Obi sat for his G.C.E. Ordinary level. When the results came, it justified all the efforts and sacrifice. He passed in five papers at the credit level. He was overjoyed. The news gave his mother a new spirit. She hoped for a day when Obi will go to one of the Universities. She made sure she told everyone she met. Most people rejoiced with her. They saw it as an achievement on the part of this youngman who achieved what some people spent five good years in the Secondary schools with all things provided and still could not attain.

Armed with his new certificate, Obi soon began bargaining for a new and better job. He wrote applications. They were promptly replied but not without the "Kola" and some connections. Two months later, Obi landed a job with the Continental Supply Company as an invoice clerk. It seemed nature was at last smiling at him. The conditions of service were excellent. The prospects were brighter. Obi settled on his new job. He had high hopes. He worked to impress his boss. He was commended always for his drive and initiative.

Albeit, this was the foundation of events that changed the whole course of Obi's life. It was the beginning of the the end. Obi was sentenced to three years imprisonment with hard labour.

The three years jail term were the making of him. His Criminal tendencies matured during these years. He came out changed and determined. It was now clear to him that he had no spring-board from which to take off. No matter how hard he tried, it was an obvious fact, which he was very conscious of that much as he tried to get back to the society and mix, he would still be identified with the stain on him. He would remain and be referred to as an ex-convict, a social stigma, socially anathemized. He had been mapped out and acquired an emblem, not easily erasable.

He was resolved. The society at large owed him a score. He was prepared and determined to settle it and in his own way and time. He was prepared to take revenge on a society that had so far treated him badly and alienated him and yet offered him nothing in return. He was also not ready to mask his hatred, animosity and hostility under any appearance of friendliness. He had to dish it out cruelly. He was mortgaged to vengeance, a vengeance with a purpose.

Reflectively, his mind thought of what militiated this decision Bitter memories of his childhood flooded his mind with such ferocity that it only rekindled his hatred and avowed vengeance. It was a childhood devoid of adequate care and affection. His father's death had struck a deadly blow on the family. It appeared as if the entire family had died too.

His uncle became very mischievous and avaricious. He laid his hands on all that belonged to his brothers, Obi's father. Obi's mother made many fruitless effort to assert her presence at least for the sake and survival of her children but it was to no avail. Every plea fell on deaf ears. The kinsmen were called in but they all felt it was prying into another man's family affairs. ''Nwodo had the right to do anything in his family,'' they contended. The village wisemen had no solution to her problems either, justice was delayed at least to the time her children would be old enough to speak for themselves. After all, she was a widow and had little authority to fight a custom that left no place for a woman to fight for property, where she herself was equally regarded as one.

Obi was still in his second year in the secondary grammar school. He knew that he had little or nothing to say.

Each night, in the seclusion of their little hut his mother would tell her son her ordeal in the hands of Nwodo his brother-in-law.

"Mama, don't worry, when I become a man, I will deal with all of them. That Uncle Nwodo is a wicked man." Obi will always say in his childish heroism.

"My son, just pray to God always. If we have God, we have all.'

"Okay, mama."

Obi had one obsession. That of making his Uncle smart for this injustice when the time comes, and getting back all that rightly belonged to his father. He had hardly had time for this when nature flagged him down. Little did he realize what nature had in stock for him. The jail term doomed him. This made him less acceptable within the community at large. He now had no right to stand in the village square to speak and argue for his cause and a just one too.

Reasons that preponderated over other consideration was the sentence. He was convicted for a crime he knew absolutely nothing of. He was only a scapegoat, a sacrificial lamb, a victim of circumstance, a defenseless martyr that had to suffer and die for others to live and enjoy.

Once again like in the past years, his mind flashed back to the events that brought this remarkable and astronomic change in his life. The one single factor that turned the table against him.

Three and half years ago, he was an invoice clerk with the Continental Supply Company Limited a Multi-National Company with opportunities for an enterprising youngman such as he was. Hardly any working day passed without Obi making twenty naira in the least from tips he got from customers. People who wanted a favour from him, those he had done a favour, those who hoped to come to him for a favour in the nearer future. It was called "We sting the ground" and everyone understood. Nobody grumbled or complained.

At the end of every month, he found himself making twice his monthly salary of a hundred and fifty naira. With these, he was able to take care of the family, a responsibility saddled on him with the death of his father. He was able to pay the school fees of his brothers and a sister in the secondary boarding school conveniently and still lived comfortably. Recently, he gave money for the commencement of moulding of cement blocks to replace the thatch house in the compound which was the only legacy left for them by his avaricious uncle out of what belonged to their father.

News of his progress permeated the village. Every one marvelled at the progress he was making. He could not agree better. Most of the time, he found himself wondering as well. His was the proverbial cow that had no tail but had God to help drive away flies. His experiences as a boy prepossessed him towards taking a different outlook towards life. He never forgot whose son he was, as his father would always hammer upon before his death.

He came from a society, where keen rivalry among peer groups in terms of wealth acquisition was the order of the day, your background notwithstanding. Where emphasis was no more laid on academic glory but on material acquisition. A place where the word "golden fleece" had lost its meaning. Many youngmen had been led to crime in order to meet the demands of this society. You become a Chief and a man of the people if you had money. No matter your virtues, they were dead if there was no money to back them up.

It was in this society that Obi found himself. Despite his poor upbringing, he still stood his grounds in the midst of his group. He was grateful to God almighty. His mother was always proud of him and exaggerated the little presents Obi occasionally sent home.

Things had been going on like this for over two years since he had been in the employment of the Company until one fateful Friday afternoon. Obi was about closing for the day when a man in black suit with a hand plaited tie, black shoes, strode into the office. He was clutching a Continental briefcase the type that bore big holes in the pay pockets of Clerical Officers. He dressed as if he was advertising the latest from the 'mens' in a fashion house.

Obi looked up at the approaching figure and continued on his job. When the man got nearer his table, he gave a slight tap on the table.

"Good afternoon, Mister."

Obi looked up again from the maze of invoices that sprawled on his table at the man. He was dressed impressively. He was his type of man. Obi dressed well and liked men who had a nice taste in clothes. He therefore on account of that made up his money to help him out.

"Good afternoon Sir! Yes! can I help you?"

"You are Mr. Ibe."

"Yes! please sit down. Just a moment." The man sat on a chair opposite Obi and watched as he ransacked through the invoices scattered on his table. He was in no hurry. He was here for a business and would remain as patient as the vulture. His mind seemed removed from the present. He was only thinking of the 'deal' ahead. If it materialized, he would buy himself a Mercedes Benz car for Christmas. Obi was his means to this end. He had watched him for the past three months with keen interest, sent people to offer him tips.

Obi was too engrossed in his search for an invoice that he momentarily forgot the presence of the man sitting opposite him. The only thing that reminded him of the man's presence was the rich odour of the perfume that filled the room. The invoice he was looking for was all that mattered to him. It would fetch him a "murtala" from a customer who wanted the photostat copy. That was primary, every other thing was secondary. He had nothing for the weekend, and that was his last hope. Business had been dull for that day. To him every other thing must wait "A bird in the hand is worth two in the bush." All these thought merged with his search.

After fifteen minutes search, Obi found the invoice he was looking for. He heaved a sigh of relief. He extracted it from the bunch and carefully tugged the invoice into his breast pocket and looked up at the man. Now for matters of the moment, he thought with a satisfied smile to the man.

"Oh! Please I am sorry for delaying you."
Yes! what can I really do for you?"

"Never mind." The man flashed back a smile. He extended his hands to Obi and Obi took it. It was masculine and adorned with gold bracelet and an Omega gold wristwatch. He held Obi's hand a second too long, wanting him to record and appreciate the ostentation. It spoke for itself, affluence and wealth. Obi realized it too and flashed him more smiles.

"I am John Ade, a businessman," he allowed that to sink in. "A friend of mine recommended you to me as a nice and understanding youngman," he paused. Before Obi could say anything, he continued. "By the way, when are you closing for the day?"

Obi glanced at his wristwatch. It was already twenty minutes past five o'clock.

"I was about closing when you came in."

"Are you free for the evening?"

"Em! not quite. Well it all depends on what you mean. I have a date at 8.00 p.m."

"What about a bottle over there at the "Highlife?"

"I don't mind."

Most often, Obi saw it as a discourtesy to refuse offers for a drink not to talk of when the month had reached the twenties, a time when one could hardly afford to have three bottles at a sitting without having to starve. This was a drinking scholarship. He hurriedly locked up his drawers and straightened himself.

"I am set."

Both left the office. At the gate, the man saw the office messenger who showed him in and gave him a ten naira note. The messenger squealed with delight. He also gave five naira to the gateman.

"Sanu! Ranke Dede!" shouted the man.

All these were done to impress Obi. Obi knew it. Without denying it, he was actually impressed. He was carried away by the man's display of naira. If this man can afford to give away fifteen naira in a flash to a messenger and a securityman, he, Obi was sure to attract something much more, at least twenty naira he thought. This could be a manna from heaven. His mind swam off with what he would do with money that weekend. He immediately remembered Toyin, his Yoruba girlfriend and her insistent demand to go and watch a show at the National Theatre. Ten naira for a double ticket. Up to that moment, he had only three naira on him and a hope for a twenty naira from the customer who wanted the photostat invoice before this man dropped in from nowhere. This was luck smiling on him.

When they got to "Highlife" the place was fully-packed with the early weekenders. Most offices had closed for the weekend. Everyone was talking at the top of his voice as if trying to outtalk his partner. Young girls who patronized the place were seen in all shapes and forms, some were almost nude and with obnoxious smiles. All were trying to outwit one another in the mechanical swaying of their buttocks to attract the prospective customers. Most people were either busy drinking their beer or at the slot machine popularly refered to as "Kalukalu" piling the machine full with coins with such an unbelievable speed as if the coins were hurting them. They were all struggling to off load their money into the machine for the Lebanese man's routine collection the next day. Some could be seen sweating in the air conditioned gambling room after turning their pockets inside out. The juke-box was playing a tune from Fela's 'Jeun ko ku.' It was loud and harsh and it pierced the ears. Giggles of young girls on the laps of their drunken men could be heard. There was a babal of voices which merged with the strident notes of the music to make the atmosphere charged and disagreeable.

They searched through the crowd and eventually found a seat at a far corner just for two and sat down. That suited Mr. Ade, at least he needed the privacy to enable him execute his plans. He beckoned to the waiter. When the waiter came, Mr. Ade looked Obi in the face and smiled.

"I am sure you must be hungry. I am hungry myself. I have not had anything today. It happens so, more so when you are in business, you seem to forget hunger. Hope you won't mind."

Obi just smiled at him.

"What would you have?"

"Rice and fried plantain." replied Obi.

"And maybe with 'club beer' to wash it down the drain," he laughed hilariously. Obi just smiled in confirmation. Mr. Ade ordered for two plates of fried rice with plantain, two chickens and four bottles of beer.

While they were waiting for their orders to arrive, Obi tried to appraise this man. What could he be wanting from him to warrant this ostentatious festivity. He started becoming apprehensive and sceptical about this man's intentions. He prayed that whatever it was, it should be what he could accomplish without any jeopardy to his job. He had a moral duty to do what he accepted a tip for. He saw no justification in accepting tips for what one could not do. It pricked his conscience. Just then, his thought was interrupted.

"Obi, tell me how long you have been on this job with this establishment?"

"I will be two, next month."

"Please tell me Mr. Ade, which friend of yours recommended me to you?"

"Oh! Never mind, he likes to remain anonymous."

Just then, the waiter arrived with the loaded tray and the bill. Obi saw the upturned bill and looked away. It read twenty-four naira. Mr. Ade brought out wads of Naira notes mainly of the twenty naira denomination for Obi's eyes to see and appreciate. He extracted a twenty naira bill from the middle and got a five from his hip pocket and handed them over to the waiter.

"You can keep the change."

"Thank you, sir."

"Go ahead, feel free please," he said to Obi.

"Thank you"

Obi descended on the food the way a dog will snap at a bone. Obi, because of the load of work in the office did not have his lunch that afternoon. The presence of the food and its delicious aroma made him more hungry. He ate ravenously in silence. It was a sumptuous meal. It was a change from Mama Iyabo's 'bukar' stuff which served the company, Obi devoured the food. After the

meal, he heaved a sigh of satisfaction. The waiter came promptly
and cleared the table. The effect of the tip was still working on him.

They poured beer in the glasses toasted each other.

"Cheers."

"Cheers."

They had a long sip and placed the glasses on the table.

"How much do you earn monthly, Obi?"

"Pardon."

"I said what is your monthly salary?" Obi stared at him. He
felt that this was an intrusion into his private affair. His salary
was his problem and nobody's. But not wanting to offend this
August spender, he inflated his salary, at least to raise his ego.

"One-eighty."

"You see, I can't imagine how a young man like you could live
on that meagre salary. Maybe your parents are very rich and you
have no responsibilities."

Obi's mind raced home to his mother and brothers and sisters
at home.

"Not at all. My parents are not rich and I have responsibilities."

"Why then do you stay on? You are young and promising. You
are the type I would like to help out of poverty if they could co-
operate. I am a businessman with various connections. Getting a
better paid job for you will be no problem."

"I will be delighted."

"You look enterprising. That is why I am making you this
offer."

"Would you like to be my business partner?" Obi did not
answer. He looked at the man. How could he be a business partner without money? What type of business does not require money?

"Well, I know what you are thinking of," said Mr. Ade. "You
are afraid of the financial side of it. Is that not so?"

"Look, you don't need to contribute to the capital. In fact this
business needs little capital. It only entails your using your number
six. It is more of brain work."

"How?" Obi was still in the dark.

"For instance, if you are ready to co-operate, we can make
money in your company without anyone getting hurt, you and I."

"Not clear please, I don't understand what you mean by making money from my company."

"Okay, let us look at it this way. Assuming you can give me specimen signatures of the signatories in your company, and an invoice booklet, all you need to do will be to sit back and relax and money will be flowing in for you. By the time you get those things, you must have completed your side of the assignment. What about that for a start?"

Obi started to shiver with fright. He spilt his beer on his trouser. This was nothing but defrauding the company. Something he had never dreamt of. He became scared of the man sitting opposite him. If any man could think up this, he was capable of killing to carry out such a scheme. His religious upbringing had a firm grip on him for him of indulge in such criminal act. He was not quite satisfied with the present state of things. He tried to sip the beer to steady his nerves but it tasted sour. He placed the glass on the table his hand shaking. He looked at the man fixedly and stood up. He was determined to leave there. So the man with whom he had been sitting and drinking was a dupe?

"Mr. Ade, if I had the courage, I should have handed you straight to the police. But-----"

"Look Mr. Ibe---"

"I am sorry I have to go. You picked on the wrong person," Obi cut in.

"Look Mr. Ibe, sit down and don't be too irrational in your decisions. Be of your age. Reporting me to the police will not benefit you. It is your word against mine. Like I told you, I have connections everywhere. Listen, these days, nobody gets rich your ideal way. No money is ever hot when it is either in your account or in your pocket. If you are fast, you make money. If you are dumb you remain poor. There is nothing like soiling your hands. Your monthly salary cannot take you anywhere. You are completely dead in the society without money, remember that. All I need from you is an invoice booklet and specimen signatures and you have nothing less than ten thousand naira in your account before two weeks. That is much more than your salary for five years.

"Look 'Mr. Man', I still maintain you picked on the wrong man for your deal. Your proposition is quite good. I appreciate your concern for me, but I am sorry I can't help you. I am satisfied with the little I earn and besides, it is criminal."

"Look Obi, You might regret it. This is an opportunity of a life time. You take it and you scale through many odds, leave it, you regret. I have not much to say."

Obi stood still, anger swelled in him. He felt like punching this man straight on the face. But for better judgement and decency he walked away. The man walked after him.

"Look youngman, you will have yourself to blame. Do not say I did not tell you." Obi ignored him and walked on, when he got to the road, he waved at a taxi.

"Shomolu two naira."

"Enter."

Slumped on the back seat of the taxi, Obi's mind dwelt on his encounter with the Businessman. Most of these so-called businessmen are robbers in disguise. They dress gorgeously and carry expensive briefcases, fake business cards with no office address, looking for somebody to sink with them in their ignoble profession. He was first taken aback by the way the man spent. Surely he did not work hard for it. He felt convinced that he was not going to regret anything. It was an empty threat to cajole him into accepting. In as much as he worked conscientiously, no harm would come to him. He wanted to get rich, make a name for himself but not to get rich through devious ways.

Three weeks after Mr. Obi's encounter with Mr. Ade, the monthly stock taking produced shocking results. Goods worth thirty thousand naira had disappeared from the warehouse. The Stores Officer reported to the Director. Everywhere was on fire. Investigation started. All documents were checked and cross checked. All signatures were scrutinized.

At long last, it was discovered that Obi signed the documents with which the goods were taken away from the warehouse.

As soon as Obi got to the Office the following morning, the Director sent for him.

"Good morning Sir." said Obi as he walked into the already opened office with the Director pacing up and down the room.

"Obi."

"Sir."

"Are you aware of the results of the stock-taking we had two days ago?"

"Yes Sir."

"What do you know about it?"

"I heard that some goods were missing from the store. I have been wondering about it too."

"What then do you know about the missing goods?"

"I don't understand you, Sir."

"You don't understand me? Who signed this invoice?" he shouted at him trusting the invoice on his face.

Obi kept mute. He was confused. What on earth was this Director driving at? He stood there, trying to piece things together, since he did not sign any invoice, he never cared to look at it. But the realization of the accusation stung Obi like a bee. He picked up the invoice, truly it was his signature. He was stunned. He became shaky not with guilt but with the thought of the stain it will give to his reputation. He raved wildly with anger, but remembering the hopelessness of the situation he found himself in, he managed to calm down and held himself together.

"Excuse me Sir, I don't understand what you are trying to insinuate, but I still maintain that I don't know anything about the missing goods, neither did I sign and stamp any invoice, anybody could have signed the documents."

"Maybe I did," interjected the Director.

"I didn't say so, but all what I am saying is that I don't know anything about it."

"If you claim you are not, who else did it. You have the official stamp, the signature on the invoice is yours. You are the only person authorized to sign invoices when I am not in. Maybe you will explain better when the time comes." He shouted and stormed out of the office, red with anger.

Obi sank in his seat when he got back to his table. He was perspiring heavily. He brought out his handkerchief and mopped his face. He was in grave danger. He was sensible of it. He knew that pleading ignorance was no solution, it will not save him. In as much as his signature was found on the invoice and it was his schedule of duty, he was to be held responsible. He picked up the copies of the invoices the Director had thrust on him and examined the signatures the second time, they were the exact replica of his, but he was sure he did not sign them. Who else did? The Director's questions re-echoed in his mind. Someone must have forged his signature. Someone within the office. Was there anyway of salvaging his reputation, image and job? If he could lay his hands on the culprit. But how? No one would be so bold, so insensible to come and admit such a hideous crime, fully aware of the repercussions. What sort of ill-luck was this? At a period when his life was just trying to take a pattern. Two weeks ago he was recommended for a promotion. This ignoble accusation if not sorted out before the next board meeting will not only mar his prospects, but would definitely throw him out of his job and worse still see him behind bars. He stood up lazily. When he looked at his wristwatch he was suprised. It was already past six o'clock. He rushed to the toilet and washed his face, when he looked into the mirror, the figure that stared back at him was ghostly. It had melancholy written all over. He ran the comb soullessly through his hair. When he got back to the office, it was then that he realized that he was the only person left in the office.

He locked his drawer and doors and left. Even as the night watchman waved to him, Obi was miles away in thought and only nodded. He was engulfed in his thinking, all energy was drained off him. He walked but without life in him. He was melancholic. He had reached a crossroad in his life. His sun was setting at such an early age. He saw the crowd. They just walked past him. They all belonged to the group that wanted to see his end. He hated all of them. It was with great effort that he arrived home.

When Obi got home, he was far from being at ease. He could not eat nor take his regular one bottle of beer daily after work. He locked himself up and laid on his bed. The presence of anybody irritated him. He rolled restlessly on his bed.

His mind focussed on his relationship with everyone in the office. He had been very careful in the type of friends he cultivated. He had been very polite to the few who did not fall into his circle. He had also always shied away from such behaviour that could only reflect discredit upon him. Even though he accepted tips from customers, he had always been cautious and discreet in the way he did it. He never asked for tips, rather, he was given willingly.

He was completely ignorant of this offence and was riled that no one would believe his story. This depressed him a great deal. He was undergoing a mental agony. His thoughts ran hay-wire. He had always been punctilious in the performance of his duties. He had not crossed swords with anyone nor think of anyone he owed a grudge. He could therefore not understand why anyone, because of a personal and selfish end would put him into such a serious calamity. It was a mystery to him.

Here he was, his whole life plans, ambitions and aspirations being punctured and dashed against the wall. All stuck in the mud in the voyage to survival. He saw his vision of wealth and success collapsing. This was nature playing tricks on his destiny. He considered what might be the fate of his younger brothers and sisters, no one could as yet stand on his or her feet and his aging mother. The thought shook him. If the culprit was not found, he was surely going in for it.

He considered the enormity of the allegation. Giving away, signing and stamping invoice with which goods worth thirty thousand naira was made off with was no joke. He knew it was an inside job. He knew somebody within the company must have a hand in it, but who? The answer eluded him.

He connected it with the visit of the unscrupulous businessman, Mr. Ade. He was surely responsible for this. How could he get at him? He did not get his address and he felt sure that if he had asked for it it would have been fake. This is misfortune pursuing him.

He was sensible of the danger he was in. That was why he had refused to yield to Mr. Ade's proposals even though they were tempting. He knew that any hitch could be traced back to him.

He had at all times avoided indiscrete behaviour which might give anyone a handle against him. Though he could not think of any, he still believed the world was a unique place where enemies were cultivated without the slightest provocation or cause. Now, he had got to answer for an offence he neither committed nor knew something of.

He tried to think up within the establishment who could have done it, somebody whose intrigue has landed him in this great difficulty? The messengers?, the cleaners? other clerks? The Director himself? The more he thought of it, the more confused he got. After about ten minutes of fruitless effort, he gave up the attempt in despair. All of a sudden his memory jibbed completely. Dozed off to a troubled sleep filled with nightmares and hallucination.

It was already twilight when Obi woke the following day. The early morning December sun pierced his window playing on his face. He staggered up from the bed and put off the radio he had left on the previous night. He ran out of his room for the bathroom for a quick shower, when he got there, the queue of tenants waiting to take their turns was too much for him to wait. He ran straight to the tap and washed up his face and legs. Within five minutes, he was hurriedly dressed and locked up his doors.

A kilometre and half from Obi's house on his route to the bus-stop, the Apostolic Church of the temple of the Lord was in full swing with their choruses. Clapping and dancing, their feet stamping and resounding joyously. Each member's worries buried, swallowed and forgotten momentarily.

Obi worshipped in this particular church every Sunday. He never missed out a single Sunday. When he first heard the singing and clapping from afar, he thought it was the normal morning worship. But on getting nearer, he saw it was the full Sunday service.

In his disturbed state of mind, he had been too consumed in his thoughts to remember that the day was Sunday and a work-free day for him. He stopped in his track and turned and started walking back home. He dodged to avoid being spotted by any member of the church. When he got home, he opened his door and slumped on his bed. He was not in the mood. Two streak of teardrops meandered through his face and ended their journey in his mouth. The salty taste of the tears made him shiver. He stood up and banged the door shut with such force that it shook the building.

He resumed his brooding not in a definite pattern but scattered thoughts. Thoughts of suffering and torture swept through his mind.

Obi remained locked-up throughout the day, even persistent knocks on his door by friends which attracted the attention of his co-tenants never made him open up. He wanted very much to be alone and think. His only companion was his beer. He drank all day through from the supply in his little therma-cool refrigerator. That helped steadied his nerves. He considered the case in all its ramifications. He looked at the alternatives opened to him. The one thought that kept coming back to him was the urge to run away, run to the east and hide, where no one will ever find him. But that will be tantamount to accepting guilt and at the same time involving his two referees, he thought. Consequently, he became determined to see the case through. By eight p.m., Obi slipped into a drunken and dreamless sleep.

Obi woke up with a start. The early morning Moslem call for worship by the Imams were all over the air. He was lucky when he got to the bathroom that nobody was there. He had an undisturbed bath. By 6.00 a.m., he was dressed and left for work.

The heavy traffic along Murtala Mohammed Way was at its worst. The vehicles moved at snail speed. This gave Obi time to rehearse what he had prepared to tell to the Director. But as he got down at Idumota bus-stop and saw the office buildings, his courage faltered, his heart missed a beat. Remembering the Director's threat, he wanted to turn back and run. Just then, he saw the Director's car drive past him. He stopped short. He stood transfixed, perhaps for a second or more. He was lost in deep thoughts.

The blasting of car horns and curses on him by irate drivers brought him back to the present. He walked to his office. When he got in everyone looked at him. He felt their eyes boring holes through him. He went to his seat and sat, his face tense with anxiety and expectation.

Before the close of work on Saturday, words had passed round on the invoice and the missing goods, and other documents and Obi's purported involvement with exaggerations. Though most of them did not know the details of the case, yet many were ready to vouch for him. They had always seen him as a transparently honest, reliable and hardworking young man.

No sooner had he arrived than the Director sent for him. When Obi saw the messenger approaching him, he knew instantly and was already up before he got to him. Courteously, Obi tapped on the Director's door and eased it open. Sitting beside the Director as he got in was a man.

"Good morning, Sir."

"Good morning, Mr. Ibe. Please do come in and sit down." Indicating an empty chair opposite them. When Obi sat down, he looked at the men with great scrutiny and his eyes finally settled on the other man. He looked every inch a cop. Obi fidgeted.

"Mr. Ibe, here you meet Detective Inspector Victor Ajayi from the Criminal Investigations Department. He has come to help us sort out some minor problems within the establishment. I am sure you will do your best to cooperate with him." The threat of yesterday was no more in his voice. Having worked in Lagos for twenty-two years, he knew it was possible for one's signature to be forged and used in such dubious circumstance. He had been a victim once, but was lucky that the culprit was caught before much damage was done. Also, having worked with Obi for almost two years, he was ready to vouch for his innocence. But then how does he explain it to the Board of Directors. How he had wished Obi was not involved. In this case, his hands were tied.

"Well, Mr. Ibe," Inspector Ajayi cleared his throat. "As your Director had just said, within your establishment, there is a reported case of fraud, all indications point to you. Take a look at this signed invoice. Is that signature yours? I mean the signature which the storeman will always recognise as yours."

Obi looked again at the invoice. It was exactly his signature, no doubt about it. "Yes, sir."

"What do you know about the missing inovice, this signature and the cleared goods?"

Obi looked at the man, then again at his Director and remained dumb to the question.

"Look youngman, regard us, your Director and I as your friends. We will do everything we can to help you. Try and co-operate."

"Sir, between you, me and God, I don't know anything about all what you are saying. Though these signatures look every inch my own, but I swear I did not sign them neither did I stamp nor collect anything from the warehouse."

"We are not saying you collected the goods from the ware-house, but somebody you know, maybe some of your friends must have and with your assistance. We want them. These names and adresses."

"Sir, I don't know anyone."

Inspector Ajayi looked sideways at the Director, and indication that the interview wasn't going to get anywhere and should be cut short. He stood up and turned to Obi.

"Maybe you will accompany me to the Headquarters. Mr. Direc-tor, we shall send for you when we want you."

"Alright Inspector Ajayi and thank you. I am at your beck and call."

As soon as they arrived at the Police Station, Obi was booked. He was taken to the interrogation room. The only furniture in the room, was a small wooden table with two chairs.

"Obi, think it over, I will be right here in an hour's time." said Inspector Ajayi."

As the door closed after the Inspector, he heard the turning of the key. Obi burst in tears. He could not believe all this was hap-pening to him. Where was God. Will God allow all this to happen to him, and allow the culprit to get away with it. Why not one of those miracles to happen, the culprit owning up and him, Obi, set free?

He remembered the story told by a friend of Paul's years back when he was still unemployed. They were discussing about heavenly judgement. The friend had argued that if God had been meting out instant justice than waiting for a particular day in heaven, the world would not have been corrupt. One who remembered that his judgment would follow immediately would dare not commit such a crime.

A friend to a friend of Paul was given a taxi by a friend to ply the roads in the far North against the advice of other friends and relatives. Having much trust in this driver friend, also trying to show gratitude for a favour done to him when things weren't okey, gave out this taxi but never failed to tell the taxi driver friend the decision of other friends and relatives. The driver promised to shame his detractors.

But as ill-luck would have it, exactly three weeks after this car was bought. A man approached the Taxi driver for a charter ride to and from a village Thirty kilometres away. He promised it would never take time. To compound things, he offered him what he got for half of a day, twenty naira. The unsuspecting driver accepted jubilantly. They set out for the journey.

Truly, they got to the man's destination, within twenty minutes, the man finished the said business and came out smiling at the driver. Off they drove back towards the town. This made the driver less cautious. He seized all fears. He wished such quick jobs would always come his way.

After fifteen kilometres drive, they came to a small village. The man asked the driver to stop. He begged for a favour. Now that he was near, would the driver oblige him to see his sister just for five minutes. The driver glanced at his dashboard clock. He still had time. The whole journey so far had not taken him two hours.

"Okay," he said.

"But first, before I forget, take your twenty naira." He counted out twenty naira from a bunch and handed it over to the driver. This dispelled whatever suspicion he had.

"Thank you sir. Where does your sister live?"

"Just branch to that untarred road by your right."

The unsuspecting driver branched off. He drove in for almost five kilometres before meeting the first house.

"That is the house."

As he stopped, the man went in and emerge after three minutes.

"I am okay, now we can go."

Three kilometres ahead, he complained about a bad stomach.

He pleaded with the driver to allow him enter the bush and empty his bowels. That never looked suspecting. The driver agreed.

The man had just finished and was inside the car when the driver felt like doing the same thing.

"Oga make you no vex o, me too wan go do wetin you do."

"Ha! No problem, but don't waste time. I have an urgent business to attend to in town."

The driver rushed off to the nearby bush, but made a fatal mistake. He left the ignition key in the car. If it was the key that made the man do it or he had original intentions about snatching the car, no one could really tell. But what happened next was that the car zoomed off.

The drive clutched his trousers and ran out in bewilderment. He shouted, but the screeching of the tyres drowned up his voice. He ran back to the house they had come from but they claimed they did not know the man. He ran back to the tarred road.

His first action was to run to the town and report to the Police. When he got there, the chase car had no petrol in it. He was therefore asked to find a car. He rushed to the motor park. He was just concluding the negotiation for a taxi for the chase, when a taxi driver friend of his saw him and shouted, "Old boy how manager?'

"Bo, they have stolen my taxi."

"But is this not the number of your taxi?" He showed him a number written on a piece of paper. "I saw it crashed into a tree at kilometre fifteen and the body of the driver is lying down there. I thought it was you. I was just about going to your people to report the accident."

"It is the body of the thief."

To Obi, that was instant justice. Would it happen in his own case?

Just then he heard the turning of the key.

Detective Inspector Ajayi walked in and drew a seat nearer Obi and sat down.

"Mr. Ibe, since you maintain you were not the one who signed it, do you know of any one who might want to implicate you? I mean is there anyone you have in mind that might have given you away?"

Obi gazed at the wall as if expecting the answer to be written there.

"Okey, do you have anything to tell me that might help you?"

"Three weeks ago," Obi started. "A man came into my office and invited me out. He made a proposition to me which I refused."

"What was the proposition?"

"He asked me to get him some specimen signature from the office and an invoice booklet."

"Did you get it for him?"

"No I refused."

"What was to be your reward for this?"

"He promised me ten thousand naira."

"Ten Thousand naira? "But that was tempting enough. Why didn't you agree?"

"Sir, first, I am quite satisfied with what I earn, secondly, I am a Christian and doing that would be sinful. It will also damage my image. My people will surely ask where I got such money from."

"But are your saying that Christians don't like money? I am a Christian myself and I like money."

"Not that type of money. I did not earn it and I might be putting others into trouble."

"But now, someone has put you in trouble."

"God will pay him back."

"Okey, when this man came to you with such fantastic offer, did you report to your Managing Director or to the police?"

"I didn't."

"Why?"

"I felt that by my rebuffing him, he would not try it with the company. Also I felt I had handled him well."

"Can you trace the man?"

"No, Sir."

"You mean you don't have his address or anything about him?"

"I left him in annoyance. But if I still see him I will recognise him."

"That is ten to one chance."

"Mr. Ibe, could you please put all this in writing and sign it?"

"Yes, Sir."

Obi wrote his statement and signed it.

For two days, Obi remained locked. Nobody came forward to bail him. On the third day, his absence was reported to the Chairman of his town Union who on enquiry got wind of Obi's detention. An emergency meeting was summoned. On the fourth day, Obi was bailed after the completion of all necessary formalities. While out, he was patient, uncomplaining and endured all sufferings and humiliations with perseverance, hoping that before long a deliverance was bound to come to judgement. He prayed fervently. Special praying sessions were organised by member of his church. He still believed in God and his wonderful works of mercy and his defence of the defenceless and oppressed.

A week later, Obi was arraigned before the court. Charged with fraudulently collecting goods of the company worth Thirty-five Thousand naira with some other people at large. A day before, Obi's mother had arrived from home to come and witness the trial of her son. The proceedings were not very elaborate. The invoices were tendered as exhibits. Witnesses were called in. The store's officer testified. His Director also testified. The whole evidence was against him. Nobody knew the facts of the case not even the accused.

His lawyer pleaded the innocence of his client; his was a case that required mercy. He was a victim of circumstance and felt very sure that the culprit was just by the corner.

Three weeks later, the case was dispensed with and Obi was found guilty of fraud. He was sentenced to three years imprisonment with hard labour.

There was a revulsion of feeling in favour of Obi by those present in the courtroom as a result of the sentence. Everyone saw innocence written on the face of this young man as he stood on the dock. Even the trial judge felt it, but it was circumstantial evidence against him. The course of law must prevail.

During the months that intervened, his mother bore all sufferings, gossipings and humiliations with fortitude. She exhibited an unspeakable calm and courage. She hoped for the day when her son would complete the three years jail term. But six months later, tragedy struck, she died of heartbreak. She was driven almost insane with grief. She had cried wringled on the court floor, crying her son's innocence as he was being led away to the black maria for his journey to the maximum security prison. But that had not been enough to revert the sentence or the mind of the learned and impartial judge. She only succeeded in attracting public sympathy for his son. But it was not strong enough to alter the course of his destiny.

Three years had come and gone. Obi once more found himself a freeman. This time, with a difference. He felt exhilarated as he walked out of the walls of the maximum security prison.

Immediately he left the prison, he made straight to the house of his friend Uche. There was a common bond between them, almost greater than that which existed between brothers.

Uche had shown great sympathy during Obi's trial. He was always at the court on time. It was he who arranged for the lawyer. When Obi's mother came, Uche took care of her and even paid her fare home. This was in appreciation of Obi's help to him. It was Obi who brought him to Lagos, accommodated him and even got a job for him. When he felt dissatisfied with his first job, Obi with his connections got him another job. Such was the relationship that Obi's first thought was to go to Uche's house. He hoped to stay with him for sometime to get settled and make plans for the future.

When Obi left the prison, he hopped a bus for Ajegunle a town at the outskirts of Lagos metropolis. Inside the bus, he felt very strange. He felt everyone looking at him or so it seemed. Why should everyone just stare at him as if he was an ape from the prehistoric days? Was there any emblem attached to him indicating that he was an ex-convict? When he was seated, he calmed himself down. It must have been his imagination.

At 'Peoples' bus-stop he alighted and made for Kajola Street. When he got there, Uche's door was securely locked. He started becoming doubtful if his friend was still living there. Three years was quite a time. He waited outside the yard for sometime. After about an hour when Uche did not return, he decided to go and kill time and come back later.

He knew the area so well. He went to the film house next street. The bill board had an Indian film poster on it. That was his favourite. It contained a lot of sentimentality. He paid the entrance fee and entered the dimly lit hall.

Even as he sat and watched the screen. Nothing made sense to him. He was lost in thoughts. The pictures appeared upside down. He only perceived the action by the noise made by the excited spectators. His mind was preoccupied with very abstract thoughts.

Despite all that he saw and heard while in prison, he was still determined to make a fresh start, to show the world that he had been unjustly imprisoned. He had nearly been lured into believing in crime by the various characters he met in prison, but his upbringing countered the impact it could have made on him. He would forgive the world for what they did to him. His mind plunged to the past, he assessed the present and viewed the future with a philosophical calmness. The past he thought had not been favourable, the present, well no comment; the future, unpredictable. But he hoped and prayed that it would be bright. He was only aware of the end of the film show when people around him started to mill out. He stood up, stretched himself and left with the crowd.

Back at Uche's place, he rapped gently at the door, there was nor response. He listened and heard the sound of a radio. That gave him hope. Could it be Uche or somebody else? Again he knocked. This time someone answered from within.

"Yes! Who are you?" came the familiar coarse voice of Uche.

"It is me. Please open the door."

"Wait, I am coming."

Obi was not sure if he recognized his voice but nevertheless, he was happy he let him in. As the door clinged open, Uche peeped out into the darkness. There was no light outside. Obi did not say anything. Uche's stare hardened at the face, recognition dawned on him. He looked at Obi in open mouthed bewilderment. None could utter any word. They both stood there staring at one another.

It was Uche who spoke first.

"Come in," he said, making way for Obi to enter into the room lit by a blackened lantern.

"Thank you."

When Obi came in, he looked the room over, there had not been any change in the room since the three years he had been in jail. It was the same eight-springs vono bed, now with a brownish sheet that served as a bedsheet, the same old National Transistor radio that spent twenty days of the month in a Radio Mechanic's Shop next door, the chop box that had a colour combination of oil, soot and polish and two chair's that crack even under the weight of a child of ten.

"When were you released?" he broke into Obi's thought.

"Today."

The look on Uche's face was reminiscently disdainful. It was dishonourable and scornful. Nevertheless, he maintained a discrete silence just to know what brought Obi to his house and what he wanted from him at this hour of the night.

Obi read Uche's thought instantly and decided to go straight to the point.

"Uche."

"Yes! What can I do for you?"

"I know what you feel about me. I am an ex-convict. It will be shameful to be associated with or seen with me. I represent the undesirable. But kindly allow me sometime to stay with you ———"

Uche did not allow him to finish.

He told Obi in an unequivocal terms that he was not wanted. That he could not afford to be seen together with him. It would no doubt reflect on him a dented public image. This wounded Obi's susceptibilities. Though his public rejection did not come to him as a surprise, but that it came from an intimate friend, one he had an absolute trust in was what hurt him most.

If Uche could treat him with such contempt, then nobody would accept him, he concluded. It was vain going to look for job. There would be no job. All gates will be closed, all doors shut to him. Being an ex-convict was worst than anything else one could think of. Once out, one is not given the opportunity to turn a new leaf.

In his case, he had never been a criminal. But does it matter? An ex-convict was an ex-convict, whatever made you one was immaterial. It was perpetual condemnation, he thought. The society was not ready to reabsorb you into its fold. Your friends would turn their backs to you, even your own family will behave to you like a total stranger. Everyone will treat you disdainfully. You had become an outcast, a societal taboo that need to be avoided just like the leper.

Where then is the corrective purpose of the sentence? It had only served to produce fresh criminals and harden the old ones. They now see it as a stage in the line of the career. It will remain the greatest and most fatal error of the society.

Once again, the words of Uche came to him. It represented the general view, friends, relatives, employers and the society at large.

He could not afford to be mooching about the streets aimlessly. He turned and left the room without saying a word.

Before he left the prison, his mind was undecided. Though Amadi had made an appreciable impact on him, he still wanted to find himself in the society and prove to them that he was actually honest. He had wanted to chalk away his sentence as part of that bitter experience that make life what it was. But with the shock he got from Uche, he was decided.

He walked into the airy night, cars swept past him and the beam of their flashlight occasionally falling on his face. As he walked along, his mind dwelt on the relationship he had struck with Amadi an inmate in the prison. He brought out the piece of paper he had given him incase he needed help. It had an address scribbled on it. It bore the number of a mechanics workshop at the outskirts of Gbagada. Obi was not familiar with that vicinity, but he was prepared to trace it. That was his only lead. He had no other person to turn to since he had been turned down by Uche. He could not afford to bring himself to go begging for shelter in any other persons house. He could be treated in the manner as Uche had done to him.

At the instance of his sentence, many people had disassociated themselves from him. Some even claimed that his much talked about achievement was infact made in no other way than such dubious means as he was jailed for. They were happy at his misfortune. They felt that it was nemesis that caught up with him.

Even without being told, Obi knew that the story of his trial and subsequent imprisonment must have diffused into the society with an alarming distortion. This was why he would never go to any of them. Let them have whatever impression they want about him, he was not perturbed.

Obi was attracted to Amadi because of his solitude. He was always looking pensively, brooding over his misfortunes. For the first six months, Obi did not break the ice. He refused bluntly to associate himself with anyone. He was always on his own. Though he went out with them for the manual labour, but he never engaged in their conversations as each prisoner recounted with exaggeration his cause for being in prison, always with a pledge to more crimes when released. Obi had absolutely nothing to offer.

The "Landlord" as Amadi was called because of the number of times he had been in and out of prison developed an immense interest in Obi. He saw in him the qualities that marked him a great leader. He became drawn to Obi, Obi initially shunned his friendship. With time however, he broke Obi's defences and penetrated his mind. Obi for the first time spoke about the invoice and his sentence amidst tears.

"My boy," said Amadi, "most of us turned to crime because of circumstance, I was not born a criminal. My father was a reverend gentleman. It was situation that made me one. I became one just to avenge a wrong. I still have more scores to settle and until I do so, I will remain in crime. I have been here for four and half years before you came in. I have two more years. You must bear your stay here like a man."

Their talk was cut short by the bell for the close of the day's fatigue. From that day both were always seen together. Obi's interest was greatly protected. He did less work. A foam was commandeered for him by Amadi who was even dreaded by the warders as well. This show of magnanimity further strengthened their relationship.

A week later, Obi had a visitor. It was for a brief period. When he came back, Amadi saw a distant look in his eyes. It was forlorn and dejected. He just walked past Amadi and slumped on his foam. Amadi left him. He knew that whatever news that was brought to him must have hit him badly.

Later, Amadi met him and he told him of the death of his mother. All tears were dried from his eyes. It had passed the stage of shedding effeminate tears. It was no more the effeminate Obi, but a changed and composed Obi.

It was really a shock to him. His mind reeled when he heard the news. He mourned her. She had exercised a moderate influence on him right from his childhood. She believed him to be innocent. He was sure that his mother died out of heartbreak because of his sentence for a crime he did not commit. The death of his mother was the last straw that has broken the camel's back.

Amadi was moved with pity for this young man who from all

indications appeared to be innocent of the crime he was convicted for. He philosophized at the need for perseverance and patience.

Gradually Obi began to buy some of Amadi's ideas and his interest in crime increased. Amadi became happy and took Obi into confidence. By the end of the two years for Amadi to leave, he had made an appreciable impact on him. Obi had almost graduated in his tutorials. It remained the practicals.

The six months he stayed after Amadi left reverted things. Some members of a religions sect had come preaching one Sunday. Obi listened to their sermons.

"The mercies of God are numerous" said the leader of the team. "You still have a chance to change. All what you need is Reverence to God, Obedience to your parents or elders and forgiveness to your enemies."

This preaching triggered off a chord in him. He remembered his dead parents and their moral instructions. Was he capable of forgiving all those that had a hand in this sentence of his? Well, it all depended on their willingness to be forgiven. His acceptance back to their fold will determine. He read the religious tracts over and over again. He was in a state of dilemma. Undecided between Amadi's proposals and offer and these religious teachings. Howbeit, time will decide.

As Uche turned him out that night, he knew instantly that the next person he had to turn to was Amadi. He was fully aware of the type of life he was now going to live. His mind was fully made up. He knew also that it was not a vocation for the weak and sentimental mind. The events of the past three years had hardened him. It was going to be a life in crime with vengeance as the watchword.

His mother was dead, he had lost his job and reputation. His younger brothers and sisters must be out of school for fees. His going home to them now was meaningless. He would be rejected at home, he had nothing to offer them. It would even compound things. No Uncle to turn to, no friend to rely on. Nothing else remained for him. He had lost all. He knew that every action has its prize tag. Nonetheless he was prepared to plunge into it.

First and foremost, he had to trace Amadi. Luckily, the late buses were still on, he took a bus straight to Bariga, and another to Gbagada. It took him over an hour to locate the workshop. But to his disappointment, the workshop was deserted. He became confused. Was it the hands of nature still pursuing him? What had he done? He stood there, not knowing what to do. There was nothing to indicate that the workshop had been used for six months. No junks and scraps associated with a mechanics workshop.

Obi must have stood there for an hour or more when he heard steps behind him. He quickly looked back and saw two mountains of men approaching him. He wanted to run. It was already past midnight, but realizing the hopelessness of it, he stayed and commuted himself to God in silent prayers.

He stood frightened to death as the men approached him. None took any notice of him. He watched them go into what looked like a tool's store. The beam of their powerful torchlight lit the entire surrounding. In a matter of moment, they were out. Obi saw them lock the store. They were both carrying briefcases. He watched them walk past him, still appearing not to have seen him. He was at a loss on what to do. He hazed about his next line of action. "This might be the lead to Amadi," he pondered.

He mustered up courage and walked after them. The distance between them increased as he tried to catch up with them. He started trottling after them, soon, he caught up with them.

"Excuse me, Sir."

Both men quickly turned and drew their gun pointing them at him. Obi died of fright. He was physically shaken. He failed to find words.

"Yes, what do you want?" shouted one of them as he advanced towards Obi.

"A--m--a--d--i," answered Obi in a tremulous voice.

"And who are you?"

"O--b--i,"

"Are you the young man that was with him in prison?"

"Y--e--s-- S-ir."

"Okay, what do you want him for?" Both men had by now returned their drawn guns to where it had sprang from. Obi was a bit relieved and relaxed. He quickly brought out the piece of paper

Amadi had given him.

"He said I could get at him through this address anytime I am released incase I needed his help."

"Do you now need his help?"

"Yes, Sir."

"Okay come along."

Obi could hardly keep up with their pace. He was almost running to catch up. About half a kilometre further, they stopped near a 505 Peugeot. Both men looked fugitively before ordering Obi.

"Enter." They commanded.

Obi entered the back seat. Both men sat in the front seat, their briefcases with Obi at the back. Obi wondered what could be in those briefcases that needed to be guided with guns. These were no doubt part of Amadi's syndicate.

The car zoomed off. The speed was too much for Obi to try to pick their bearing. He was too tired to even think. His greatest pre-occupation was finding something to eat and a place to lay his head.

After about two hours drive, the car eventually came to a halt in front of a desolated bungalow.

"Come down."

Obi obeyed and followed the men in, when he got in he made out the profile of three men sitting in the nearly dark room. Two of them looked like prize-fighters. The third Obi quickly recognized as Amadi.

"Good evening, Sir."

"Is that not Obi?"

"I am Sir."

"Good boy! sit down I knew you will come", "How manage! I was wondering whether you will not be able to locate the place."

"I saw these two men at the address you gave me and they brought me," he answered pointing to the two men he had come in with.

"Good, it is the work of God. Do you want anything to drink?"

"No! Thank you."

Obi could not afford to think of taking any alcohol in his present state of hunger. His stomach churned with the desire for food.

"Or may be you will want to eat first?"

Obi did not answer. Amadi took it to mean yes.

"Alison."

"Yes, Sir," an answer came from within, a dimunitive man came shuffling forward. "Take this my young man and make him feel at home. Go to my wardrobe, and get nice clothes for him to change with."

Alison eyed Obi with contempt and jealousy all mixed.

"Yes, Sir."

Obi followed him. Just as he was leaving the room, he overheard Amadi say to the men. "That boy has brains yet to be developed. If nurtured well, he will go places."

Two hours later, Obi emerged from the room refreshed. He had washed, eaten and was well dressed. He had shed the near rag he came in with and was in a woollen trousers, a T-shirt with "sky is your limit" inscribed on it. Still sitting were the two men he had met when he came in. The two men that had came in with him were gone. Obi found a seat and was promptly served with a bottle of beer. As he sat down and sipped his beer, his mind evaluated the sitting room and all that it contained. It was expensive and at the same time extensively furnished. Much money must have changed hands. When could he afford such luxury.

Amadi cleared his voice to attract the attention of Obi who was lost in fantasy.

"My son, you did well to have come and at this opportuned time, I have the honour to introduce to you my close associates. To your right is Frank and to my left is Rocky. They are the breed of men you will need to be associated with."

Obi momentarily looked from right to left and back to Amadi.

"Gentlemen, with you here, is Obi. He is the same young man I mentioned to you."

"You are welcome," they chorused.

"Thank you," returned Obi.

Things dragged on this way for a week. Daily, Obi would wake up, eat, drink and sleep. He now tried smoking. He started to put on weight. The second week brought a change. Obi began his training in earnest. In the mornings, he went for driving. It was the policy of the gang that everyone within the group should be able to handle a car. In the evenings, he was driven far into a forest for his shooting exercise. This Amadi did personally.

In less than a month, Obi became a perfect shot. He was also able to handle cars perfectly. Amadi was very happy at the progress he was making. Obi was now fully entangled in the meshes of crime. He now freely smoked marijuana. He was in it, it only remained his first time out. He had been adequately tutored in the rudiments, it remained action.

Three months after Obi came to stay with Amadi, the opening came. At least he must work for a living. He had lapsed in luxury. But it was now time for action. Amadi felt like putting Obi to test without meaning any harm. His first assignment was a car snatch. The venue was selected by Amadi but the strategy was to be entirely his. A girl was drafted to aid him. What Amadi needed was a car and nothing less. As Amadi dropped them off in his 505 Peugeot, he waved to them.

"Good luck to you."

"Thank you, Sir."

Kubura as Obi came to know had been in the gang for two years. She was a lead in most of the operations. She had a figure that sent tremors of desire down the veins of any fullblooded young man. If you pass Kubura on the way without taking a second look at her, either you had a stiff neck or your head needed re-examination by a Psychiatrist. She was strikingly beautiful. That gave Obi a source of courage. Working with such a beauty entails proving yourself to be a man.

Quickly, Obi mapped out the plans. Kubura was to wave for a lift. Obi would be out of sight. When the vehicle stopped Kubura would go in and Obi would emerge with her purse she was supposed to have forgotten. There Obi would take over.

Nothing happened for the first two hours. Some cars stopped on their own offering to give Kubura a lift but she declined the offer. It was getting dark. Traffic had thinned down to only two cars in thirty minutes on the highway. The zero hour was near.

A 505 came crashing down. It had the beam of its full light on gently. The screeching of the tyres alerted Obi for action. He was out the very moment Kubura was entering the car.

"Sister, you forgot this bag while you were sitting there."

"Oh! Thank you, Sir," still sitting in the car, not making any effort to go for the purse.

As the man made to collect the purse for her, he saw himself facing the nozzle of a gun.

"Come down." Obi shouted at him. Before he could make up his mind on what to do; put up a resistance or submit, Obi struck him with the butt of the gun. He groaned and stumped down on the seat. With the help of Kubura, Obi quickly dragged the man out of the car and dumped him by the roadside. He showed no sign of mercy. The horrors of the cell and his cause had hardened him. He reversed the car and drove off. All these happened within five minutes. As he drove off the car towards the rendezvous, his nerves were rock steady.

Needless to say that he kept his promise of vengeance. Obi became a terror. He plundered with reckless abandon. He took no pity on anyone. He lost all sentimentality. He was not always moved and was always unruffled. He carried out his assignments with great expertise. He was nicknamed "Terror" within the underworld. His actions made him universally accepted. Gangs came to him for professional piece of advice. He was meticulous when it came to planning and execution of a "deal". He became a maestro.

"Terror's" influence grew tremendously. He was dreaded by men and women of his like. He was ruthless. His mouth and face smiled but his eyes were always cold and hard like steel. This earned him a place in the hierarchy of the organization. Within a short time, he had assembled his own gang. His mob was a result of a nationwide recruitment drive for seasoned men and hardcores.

With each operation, his fame increased. He went for bigger stakes and was always successful. He never failed or hashed up a "deal" and would never hesitate to eliminate anybody that stood in his way in the process. Any member found wanting was dispensed with. He became the undisputed king of the underworld. Apart

from this, he also ran consultancy services for other mobs.

True he was clearly a young man of about thirty or there about, but his choice of words, his calm and composure in the face of grave danger clearly portrayed him as an assassin. He looked obviously a man who would brook no insurbordination or argument, and everyone knew it. In fact, it was madness to try an argument with Terror. He radiated pure aggression. He was pure dynamite. His presence inspired confidence in the members of the gang and that was accountable for the success. He exhibited a mercurial temperament. His contention was that what was worth doing was worth doing well. Truly, he made it.

For the first time since his release, Obi decided to go home. He had been away for so long. He had not met any member of his family. Not that he was not bothered, he really cared but he wanted to make money before seeing them. What was the need for a poor brother to a group of hungry and suffering brothers? He thought, with money, the time would be made up.

Poverty had split the family, each driven by the instinct for survival. Adaku and Ifeoma were forced to marry out of frustration. Ngozi had taken to prostitution to keep body and soul together and to cater for her two brothers in the secondary school. John could not finish his apprenticeship as a mechanic. He now roamed the streets. Chill penury like a colossus cast its domineering shadow over the whole family.

Obi drove into the neighbouring and more boisterous town in the evening. He booked for a lodging for the night in the only hotel in town. The cracking of the bed as he sat on them made him remember the difference between the rich and the poor. It was on a Saturday. He wanted to drive into his village in broad daylight on Sunday when he would meet most people in. He was not sure what the whole place would look like. Therefore, going in the night might be embarrassing.

When he got to the village the following morning, everywhere had altered beyond recognition since he last saw it. Everywhere was shining reflectively with iron sheet roofing from housetops in the early morning sun. Electric generators were humming their mechanical tunes from many houses. The village was boistering with life. Music blasted from loudspeakers placed outside the beer parlour that sprang up at the village square. As he took in this picture, he realized then how long he had been away.

He meandered through the crowd of people now trooping back from the church towards their compound. From afar, the thatched house he saw was redolent of hardship, suffering and sorrow. When he got there, the whole place was in ruins. No one seemed to have been there in recent years. Where then were the other members of the family? he asked himself.

He walked into the compound through the debris of the "Ovu". The rats were there to welcome him. Swarms of mosquitoes in stagnant waters in broken pots frowned at his intrusion. They all flew towards him in a protest. Network of spiders wove round him in his bid to penetrate. When he eventually passed, his father's grave stared at him in complaint for neglect. Beside the almost level earth mound was another grave which obviously was his mother's beckoning on him to come. He went towards it as if in response to the call. He bent his head in reverence and in grief. He was seeing his mother's grave for the first time. Memories flooded back. He remembered all that had happened during the past turbulent years since his father's death. He broke up. Teardrops chased themselves on his face. He brought out his handkerchief and wiped the tears off his face.

The presence of a new 505 Peugeot in the town raised a stir. No one in the village had as yet rode a car that expensive. Cars still meant eminence. The car was immediately noticed. It attracted attention, the occupant might as well be a visitor. None had seen Obi after he left the village and that was years ago. His sentence had further made them forget him. They could not therefore recognize him. Some who were doubtful could not associate the Obi they knew with such a car. But when he drove and parked in front of the compound, their doubts gave way. They all trooped to welcome him back..

"Obi."

Obi turned his head. Walking towards him was Nnanna. Nna

as Obi called him was of the same age and a playmate of his. They were always seen together. He was the only true friend Obi had after the tragedy of his father's death.

"Obi, how are you?" offering his hands.

"Fine! Thank you."

"When did you come?"

"I drove in thirty minutes ago."

"These are eyes."

"It has been a long time."

"How is life with you there at Lagos? I learnt you are in business." How is business?" Obi, since after his release had no association with anyone from the village. He was therefore taken aback at Nna's questions.

"Fine."

"How is everyone at home? You are all doing fine. Believe me. If not for my long stay in the village, I could have hardly found my way to this compound. Everywhere has changed tremendously. I like it, you know. It shows progress. Why are you at home? Or are you on leave?"

"I have always been at home. I teach in the village Primary School."

"St. Augustine?"

"Yes."

"That is lovely."

"Lovely? What is lovely in a teaching job in this state? Is it lovely to work for months without pay? Lovely to always go for credit at month ends and get ridiculed by the village folks? People who will tell you that they were all better than teachers. Lovely to suffer when your salary is being withheld by some high-handed politicians. Why does it not happen to their own salaries and allowances? Why no delay in the salary of the Governor, Commissioners or Permanent Secretaries? Why not to other Ministries? Even in the Ministry of Education, why to teachers alone?"

"Well, that makes for the difference between you and them. Your reward as a teacher, you must always remember is securely preserved for you on a table in heaven. In fact directly at the right hand side of God," Obi smiled.

"Look Obi, that was just a devise used by the white missionaries to cajole our parents into working like Jackals in what they called selfless service to God and humanity. That theory doesn't hold these days. I want my reward here, right here on earth and fast too. Are you sure I am interested in heaven?"

"It is no use standing here. You know what the village people are like. That aspect of their life has not changed. In a little while you will have the whole village on you as if you are a masquerade on display. Why not let us go to my place?"

As they left to go, Obi glanced over his shoulders to the grave and shook his head. People were already gathering outside, milling round the parked car. Obi followed his friend. They walked past the crowd. Obi nodded his head, to the crowd in acknowledgment to their greetings. Some kids still followed him.

When they got to Nna's house, Obi was led to an averagely furnished, sitting room. He quickly appraised the room and its property. At least it was not bad.

"Nna, you are not doing badly, why are you complaining? How many people in Lagos do you think can boast of having a house as decent as this one?"

"Is that the end of things? Bo what do I offer you? My wife is not back yet."

"So you are married." His eyes shone with surprise. In their hay days, Nna had always openly condemned girls and vowed to be a priest.

"So my reverend Father Nna is now married. I told you. I knew you would like them when time came. You were only shy then."

"I am a Father. Reverend or no reverend. A Father is a father. I have three kids."

"That is splendid."

"What do I offer you?"

"Do you have palmwine? I have not tasted nice palmwine for the past eight years. What we have in Lagos is a little palmwine, mixed with water and saccharin."

Nnanna quickly brought a mug of palmwine. They both settled down to their drinks. They swapped stories about their childhood pranks and jokes. It was a happy reunion.

Nna had heard much of his friend's activities in Lagos. Though he did not approve of it, at the same time, he did not condemn him outright. So far the end justified the means. Most men at the top got there through the same route. He saw no difference between an armed robber and one who swindles the state. They are all robbers. Pen or arm.

"My friend," resumed Nna.

"You have been away for a very long time, over ten years is not a joke. Many things have happened, since then. Many changes have taken place in this small village of ours. Physically as you can see, and socially. There is a new social order pervading the society. A constant struggle between the young and the old. The village square meeting no more holds. The 'Ofo' men had been reduced to ordinary old men. No one offers sacrifices to their gods. Now that you have decided to come home after your years of sojourn you must be very cautious and careful in what you do or say to them. They are our greatest enemies in this village. Your wealth will attract them toward you. But remember they are only coming for what they can extract from your pocket and mouth. They follow the tide of wealth. They are fickle-minded and your money decides where they sway to.

"As regards the death of your mother, I know how you feel about it but think less of it. What happened years ago should not bother a man of your age so much. Think about reuniting the family. Look for them and bring them together. It is your responsibility."

"Thank you Nna. I have heard all you have said. I strongly believe that nature has its own course. One's destiny is bound to be fulfilled. Whatever will be; will be. It might only take time," Obi sipped his palmwine and concluded. "Once again, thank you for the advice."

"Do you know anything about my brothers and sisters? I mean anyway to locate them."

"Yes, Adaku and Ijeoma are at home with their husbands. Udo and Bomboy are students at a Community Technical School. Emm, well, Ngozi as I learnt is responsible for their education. You know how life is hard down home. How difficult it is to make ends meet. They say she stays somewhere in Owerri, but I don't know. She will be able to tell you about the whereabouts of Kevin if you see her.''

"Thank you. Please, I would like you to get me some labourers to clear the compound. I will be back next week. Meanwhile, I would like to trace my brothers and sisters first before I decide on what my next line of action will be. I need a reunion. By the way, has your wife not returned?''

"I think she has.''

"Can I see her then?''

"Let me send for her." Just then, Nna's wife walked in. "Darling, this is Obi, my very good friend, we grew up together in this village.

"Obi, this is my wife Rose." They both shook hands and said "I'm happy to meet you.''

Five minutes later, Obi stood up ready to go. "I am going. I will drive to Owerri and from there, I will mount a search to find the rest.''

"Why not wait and eat something?'' protested Nna's wife.

"No please! thank you,'' Obi dipped his hands into his trouser pockets and brought out two twenty naira notes.

"Please Madam, take this for the kids.''

"Thank you Sir.''

Obi and Nna walked back to the car. He drove off straight to the Capital.

This behaviour of Obi left everybody dumbfounded. His uncle had rushed home as soon as he heard of his arrival and slaughtered a fowl with the vain hope that he would come in. But Obi never did. He had his plans. His contention was that a house that never welcomed him nor offered him shelter when he was in need would not contain him now.

When Obi left home, he drove straight to Owerri and booked into a hotel as a first step for the great search. A business associate of his once gave him the name of a club as a place to pick up the best lay in town, mostly school girls who wanted quick money for a new outfit to impress a peverish school boyfriend or, on-students with hobs. It has a galaxy of beautiful and innocent looking girls. The ones you would think butter would never melt in their months, yet they were worse than Jezebel, the friend had said.

The flickering neon light told Obi he was where he wanted. It read "Exclusive Cafe". Eyes were set on him as he parked the 505 Peugeot and approached the entrance to the club. At the entrance, some girls stood like wax works others talked in conspiratory tones with the men trying to strike a bargain while some sipped from a never finishing bottle by their side. Obi walked his way through the crowded room glancing about the room. He spotted a seat that had just been vacated by a couple and sat down.

Obi sat in silence for about five minutes trying to get his sight used to the room. It was in semi-darkness with a single mercury bulb dangling from the ceiling. You hardly saw who sat next to you. He was still searching for a partner with his eyes, and with Bongus Ikwue's "Searching for love" on the juke-box, you had to strain your eyes so as not to pick the wrong "love".

He ordered a bottle of beer and sipped it slowly as more of the girls trooped in. Time soon drabbed by. Not very impressed with what he saw, he went to the slot machine to kill time. The girls he saw were mostly school girls and to him, they could be great bores. Another thirty minutes went by, yet no luck. He decided to try some other joints. He would report back his findings to his friend when he got to Lagos.

As he stepped out to leave, he spotted a girl sitting all by herself at a corner of the room, she had a cigarette dangling from her mouth and cupped her glass with both hands. She sat meditatively. Something in Obi fell into place. She was talking to a friend who was leaving with a customer as he got nearer to her. There was something about the voice that sounded familiar. But then! he allowed the thought to hang.

The mercury light played tricks on Obi's eyes. The eyes of the girl was sparkling, her dress appeared to change colours as Obi fixed his gaze on them. She had the figure that moved him, slim, not too heavy burst but big enough to fill the hands and a nice waist-line. The thought gave him an erection. As he made up his mind to meet the girl, someone beat him to it. Anger swelled in him. What had he been waiting for? Feeling his erection to make sure it was real? He had missed the only thing that appealed to him by his being slow. At least all the time he used in admiring her could have been used to talk to her.

To his utter amazement, the man met with an inconceivable rebuff not akin to being given by a call girl. This gave Obi a very big relief. This action endeared Obi more to this girl, it redoubled his desire, at least it showed she was a bit discrete in the people she went out with, or would she be waiting for someone. He vowed to get her at all cost. He moved in straight.

"Good evening, sister."

"Good evening," she responded uninterestingly. Obi dangled the car key in front of her. It was a bait that most girls fall for.

"Can I talk to you in the car outside, here is very noisy." Obi stood, not quite sure of the response he would get. But as luck would have it, she put off the cigarette and stood up. Obi led the way to the impressive 505 Peugeot.

But just as they were getting nearer the car she stopped.

"I am not going near the car. The light is too much. Let us sit on these chairs."

"Okay," Obi started immediately they were seated.

"Mind my going home with you?"

"To your house?" She asked as if she never heard well.

"To my hotel, I don't live in this town. I am on a business trip from Lagos."

"I don't go with people to their places."

"I will pay for the service."

"Could it have been free before?"

"Okay before we talk, why not a bottle of beer each?"

"It is alright."

Both brother and sister sipped beer and negotiated on the price for the night. Inspite of the exorbitant amount she charged, Obi had a job convincing her to accompany him to his hotel. His extravagant spending and the car did the magic.

Most call girls prefer the security of their rooms than the unknown, more so when there were incidents of bodies of club girls picked up along the roadsides with their breasts chopped off for some kind of rituals. Rosy as she was called by her friends had never slept out since her introduction to the trade. But it was nature in one of its great roles, that made her accept to go home with this man she had never met before, a businessman from Lagos, Obi, his brother.

As they rose to go, she gave Obi her hands. Obi steered her to the car. But as nature would have it, he never tried anything. Not even trying to take advantage of her being tipsy. There was no point in rushing her. Afterall, they were going to spend the night together.

In the car, she pleaded with Obi to take her home just to inform her neighbour who was sick and would be scared if she never came back.

At the entrance to her house, she called out to Obi.

"Please come in for a minute. I want to get something for the sick girl to eat."

Obi parked the car and walked in. On the bed lay a girl who had not been receiving the best from a doctor.

"Good evening, Sir."

"Good evening sister. How are you?"

"You can see yourself," came the reply.

Up to this time, there had not been any form of introduction from Obi's side. If asked however, he would have given a wrong name.

"Please keep yourself busy with the album before I finished".

Obi took the first album. Flicked through the pages uninterestingly. He was fed up by the time he finished the first one. Pictures of young men and women in half nude positions, on bed.

"Why not look at the other album? That is mine," said Rosy, "or do I come and introduce them?"

For the desire of feeling the warmth of the girl near him, he consented.

The first picture he saw there gave him a shock. It was his own picture. It was taken during his first year in college.

"This is my elder brother Obi. He is in Lagos, but it has taken some years since I saw him last. You Lagos men, when you go out, you don't want to come back. Is that not so?"

She looked up at Obi for an answer. The look she saw on Obi's face made her jump up.

"Mr. man, what is wrong with you? Please don't faint here."
Fear seized her.

Obi looked her over as she babbled. He recognized her instantly.
"Ngozi."

Since her coming to Owerri to join the band-wagon of pro-
stitutes, no one had ever called her by that name. In fact no one
knew her as Ngozi, not even her roommate that had lived with her
for two years. She was therefore surprised. She looked closely at
Obi for the first time. She saw those rude features of his elder
brother on the man staring at her.

"Obi?"

Streak of tears meandered through Obi's face. The sister saw
the tears and knew immediately that this was Obi, her brother, she
too burst into tears. Brother and sister started crying freely. Obi
was the first to get himself together.

"Let us go."

The confused roommate watched as they both left the room.

When they got to Obi's hotel, he booked a room for his sister.
They talked far into the night. Obi tried to gather the story of the
family. To make plans. He was more than embittered now. It was
a rude awakening to reality. The society had not stopped at him
but had extended its dirty hands to his sister, turned her to a whore.
He trembled with hatred. The urge for vengeance trebled.

The next morning, they went and packed what little things she
had, and they both left for Aba. At Aba, it was not difficult
locating Kevin. He was met at the motor park, a tout. The two
brothers and their sister drove to Adaku's place. They met Adaku,
a baby on her back roasting maize in the frontage of their house.

Unlike Ngozi, she quickly recognized Obi. She jumped and clung
to her brother. Tears of joy dropping from her eyes. That night,
plans were concluded. Kevin was sent to Ijeoma, Udo and Bomboy.

A week later, Obi came back with all the members of the family as promised. The site of their compound was now cleared. Obi
held consultations with Nna. A contractor was hired to start erec-
ting structures. Joint burial date was fixed for his father and mother
to coincide with the completion and opening of the new building.

Six months later, a magnificent building stood where the ruins of their house once stood. The memorial service for his parents was held. It was very elaborate. In all, two cows were slaughtered, goats and fowls were countless. It was a befitting burial.

With time, Obi became fabulously rich. He was now lapped in luxury. He had a Volvo 244 DL., a Mercedes Benz and two Peugeot 505's operational cars. Besides, he had cosy flats scattered all over the country as hide-outs when the heat became too much or when they are on the look-out for him. He had just completed a mansion of twenty-four rooms named "Ogbodiye Lodge" in memory of his mother. It was lavishly furnished. The furniture was expensive. It has wall to wall carpeting. Everything portrayed elegance, and excellence. On entering the house, you at once perceive Obi to be a man of taste. His brothers and sisters became well of. Ngozi became a businesswoman of international repute, travelling through all the exotic cities of the world.

Many knew the source of this wealth, yet, none had the audacity to mention it. Story of Mathew, the Chairman of the Town Union Lagos branch who had the impudence to call him just a dupe during a heated argument was still fresh in everyone's memory. Mathew was locked up for days with special instructions for the police officer not to release him. It took a delegate of the Town Union and friends of Mathew to make Obi change his mind. This was a country where money meant a lot, where your life does not worth a grain if you have no money. In fact, where you are virtually dead without it.

To cover up his activities, Obi floated a private Limited company under the pseudonym of Natural Enterprises Limited. Importers, Exporters, Manufacturer's Representative and General Contractors. He got an Office and had branch Offices at his operational zones. The typist, clerks, messengers were all members of the syndicate. There were files displayed to reflect the everyday activities of a company of such, but it was all shadowy. It was under this canopy that Obi perpetuated his hideous activities. Indeed, he was a "supplier and remover".

His home-going became more frequent. It was all in a bid to carry his war of vengeance to the home front. To the place where the first rays of misfortune shone on him. It was there his problem started. Nevertheless, in most cases, he was very generous. Everytime he came home he saw the village folks flocking around him. They were at the receiving end of a dash and therefore deaf and dumb to things. Even news that filtered in from Lagos about his activities were discarded as petty jealousies of the unfortunate few who could not make it. All in all, Obi gradually made an inroad back into the society. That gave him a nice front for revenge.

Obi felt elated at the prospect of being invited to be the Chairman on the occasion of the launching ceremony of the village Community College. This was the first time he was taking part in a Community activity since recent years. To him, inviting him meant the entire village eating their words, considering what they had all said when he was sentenced and the contemptuous indifference the few whom he came across after he was released showed in Lagos. It also amounted to accepting and recognizing him. He knew that this invitation was triggered off by his donation to the Church Fund when he last visited home. He was gradually working his way back into the social life of the village. He knew it was because of his money. Nevertheless, he still decided to honour the invitation.

He arrived home a day before the launching. He used the whole of that evening entertaining business associates in his mansion who knew about his arrival.

The occasion was at its climax when Obi arrived. There was a respectable appearance. The various cultural dances were just making their exit. He arrived in his pitch black Mercedes Benz car with all its seats snowy white. It was chauffeur driven. The chauffeur was impressively dressed in a white french suit and a cap with red trimmings at its tip. Obi was also impressively and expensively dressed in a white danshiki lace and an overflowing gown. He looked stately.

He was welcomed with a rousing ovation. The driver stopped and with such an automatic alacrity came and opened the side door and stood at attention. It had a military air. Everyone turned his attention to that direction. The display was spectacular. Obi swelled with delight. His ego was magnified. He walked out with his swagger stick leaning on it as if his support lay on the stick. He was escorted to his seat on the dais by a charming lady who appeared to be walking on dunlop legs. Obi eyed her with lust.

It appeared as if he was being awaited for. The Chief Launcher, who was also the master of ceremony started off by launching the school fund with his widow's might as he called at with a sum of One Thousand Naira. There were ovations for him. Other people came in with their contributions. Individuals, clubs and various organisations in the village, all came forward, Eight Hundred, Five Hundred, Three Hundred, Two Hundred and Fifty, Two Hundred, One Hundred, Fifty naira, Twenty, Ten, Five Naira. It continued descending. Obi still kept his silence and sipped his beer gradually. The audience were worked up with expectation. People glance occasionally towards his direction. He saw them through his dark shades spectacle.

When Obi felt that the anxiety and anticipation had reached a climax and the tempo of the occasion was dying down, he beckoned on the master of ceremony. All eyes were at once turned on him. He gave himself a satisfactory grin. This was a moment he had looked forward to, a moment to create an indelible impression on the minds of everyone present. He dipped his hands into his big gown and brought out some bundles of naira notes. He had carefully counted them before he left his house. He had another five thousand naira in the car. This was for re-inforcement in-case anyone wanted to compete with him. As Obi handed over the money to the master of ceremony, his eyes shone with surprise. He called on all to keep quiet as he has a surprise packet for them. Everywhere went silent like a grave yard. They all watched as the money was being counted.

"Ladies and Gentlemen!" shouted the master of ceremony.

"It is wonderful, it is super! It is magnificent, it is sensational. An illustrious and a very important son of this village had created news, a gesture worthy of emulation by all and sundry," he paused.

Everyone was dying of anxiety to know the amount of money.

"I have with me here a sum of ten thousand naira in solid cash. Please clap your hands."

Everyone went into rhapsody over Obi's donation. There were thunderous and deafening ovation. It took the master of ceremony over thirty minutes to calm down the audience. The MC, a university lecturer went at length to eulogize on Obi's good qualities and his compatriotism.

"We owe MR. OBI IBE a debt of gratitude for his great contribution towards this fund. He has to a great extent alleviated our financial problem and reduced the burden on our old parents who pay through their sweat to see this school become a reality."

"Our children will always appreciate his immense contribution towards the academic upliftment of this village and I am sure this will be reflected in the performances in their various examinations," he concluded.

This flattery got a better control of Obi. He asked for the microphone.

"Brothers and Sisters, this is just a widow's might. Had I known that things would be as grand as this, I could have prepared well. Nevertheless, things are not bad yet. I promise to buy the iron sheets for the roofing of all the houses to be erected-----"

He did not say more than that before defeaning ovation made him sit down. More praises were showered on him.

The praises showered on Obi as an illustrious son of the village was superfluous. It lacked genuity, it was hypocritical, it was excessive and insincere. The master of ceremony and most people present knew Obi for what he was, his activities and his source of wealth. But nobody had the nerve, they dare not say anything to the contrary, else, they will invite the wrath of some people present who had been greatly impressed by his donation. Besides, no one knew to what length Obi would go in silencing anyone who summons the courage to say it out and loud. One thing was clear, the village needed the money. Ten thousand naira was not easy to come by. In fact the entire village could not have made up the amount on their own. If the church accepted the one thousand Naira he gave them, then the entire village would have no misgivings in accepting this also. Where he got the money was very immaterial, what they needed was his money and not his person.

Ade and Aduke laid on the bed. Aduke placed her hands on his hairy chest, drawing patterns. They had been like this for three hours, when she realized that time was really running out fast. It was time she talked about her birthday party, slated for next month. She had already told all other boyfriends except Ade. Though she just gave him the hint three months ago.

"Darling, you know that my twenty-first birthday comes up next month." Aduke moved closer and planted a passionate kiss on his lips. "I have assured all my friends that it is going to be big and groovy, that there would be all 'drinkables' and 'eatables' in abundance, and you know, you are the only one I have." She kissed him fully on the mouth, and looked at his face for any sign of approval.

Ade just kept his face placid. He stared at the ceiling. Only God knew how many men this bitch had roped in this birthday with same words "You are the only one" he thought. He tried to remember how old the relationship had been. It couldn't have been more than six months since he gave her the lift that eventually developed into an amorous relationship. See her now with a birthday party talk. That meant expensive presents beside sponsoring a lavish party to please her and her friends. He cursed the day he met her. What type of ill-luck pursued him, he could not tell. Any girl friend, within a short distance of acquaintanceship must either be celebrating her birthday or be burying a dead father or uncle or grandfather who died when she was not born. In each case, he had been the worse off it. That meant salary advance while his wife and three children at home bore the brunt.

As if the thought sprang him to action, he quickly threw off the cloth covering them, rose up and turned Aduke on her back. he parted her legs and entered her. Aduke closed her eyes as she saw him thrusting the fully erected manhood inside her ferociously and with such speed as if afraid it would go limp the next moment. It tore through her fiercely. Aduke gave a gasp of pleasure as she felt the whole length of him inside her. She moaned, groaned and clung tightly to Ade rocking her waist. It was like dancing in limbo. Ade pumped with alternating tempo, high and low, fast and slow. Aduke followed him in the pursuit, it was like in a rat race. Minutes later, Ade exploded with Aduke pleading No----No----don't ---- please No---No---Don't.

Ade allowed himself to drip to the last drop. Aduke held him tightly as he wanted to climb off her. With complacent smile showing gratitude she kissed him tenderly. With his "instrument" still embedded in her "aperture", he fondled her breast. She responded writhing her waist like a belly dancer. This stimulated Ade and gave him an erection once again. His immersed rod stood erect and he started the pumping all over again. If he must spend his money, he might as well start having the worth, he thought.

The thought of how to raise money for Aduke's birthday possessed him as he left in his battered Volkswagen beetle. Though the relationship was young, Aduke had been good to him. She was always there when he wanted her and never grumbled when offered paltry sum which he seldom did. There was therefore, no justifiable reason for backing out. "One good turn deserves another" they say. But how was he to get the money? That was the nagging question. At a rough estimate the party plus the present would cost more than five hundred naira, much more than his one month salary.

Come to think of it, he still had an outstanding loan to clear. Would he get a loan from the office? It is worth trying he muttered to himself. He would approach the manager first thing the next morning. With this thought, he felt satisfied. With luck on his side, the manager will approve.

The following morning, Ade approached the manager for a loan.

"Ade," the manager shouted at him. "How dare you have the effrontery to ask for another loan when you have not cleared the one you got! It is true you are hardworking. Ade, take my advice, look over your spending pattern and the type of friends you cultivate, they might lead you into trouble."

"Sir, I told you I used that loan for my father's burial."

"That doesn't erase the loan, does it? Who knows, you might need this one to bury your grandfather." He retorted. "Remember you are still owing the bank over five hundred naira. Clear that first and I will approve another for you."

"But excuse me sir......"

"Look Ade," the manager cut him short. "I have no more time to waste with you. Clear that and not until you do so, no loan for you and good afternoon."

To Ade, that signified the end of the talks. He stood up and walked out of the office dejected. "Okay! I will show this man," he soliloquized as he left the office. For the whole of the day, Ade worked with little or no concentration. Each ledger he picked refused to balance, everything he did went wrong. At the close of the day, he stumbled on an idea for a solution to his financial problem. He must squeeze out money from the bank. How? Many alternatives opened up. He considered them on their respective merits. Defraud the bank on his own or take some one into confidence. No, that might be risky. He would not like anything to be traced to him. Make some outside connection? Well, that sounded better. The foolish manager who would not be prepared to give out a repayable loan of just Five Hundred Naira should be ready to lose thousands. It only required making the right contacts and the world would be in his pocket. This thought animated him.

Initially, he dallied with the various ideas. But days later, it took enormous dimension. He saw it as the only way to an economic emancipation. If he must continue to live the life style he had cultivated, what with his chain of girlfriends, there must be money.

His service in the back had reached a high degree of excellence, at least that was evidenced by the series of promotion he had got within his nine years in the bank. He had always thought and hoped that with a step higher, his financial situation would improve. But no. It had always been the other way round. Each promotion turned things worse. With each promotion, he acquired a different standard of living not commensurate with the new status. This had always put him in the red.

Having arrived at his decision to defraud the bank, he felt no remorse, nor guilt. Though he strongly believed in the existence of a divine being, he did not actually embrace any particular religious belief. His contention was that this supreme being had created man with opportunities for advancement and survival. It was left to individuals to utilize these opportunities to their advantage. The question of which ever way it was done was quite immaterial. Men were masters of their fate. Your destiny drives through the course you channel it.

The notion of good and bad was not for him. He felt they were words created by philosophers and theologist in their pursuit to make this place Utopia. There was nothing like sin. It all depended on your state of mind. If you rightly believed that what you did was to your best interest and very important to your survival, nothing wrong in that. If one has to accept all the religious doctrines dogmatically, one would be washed offshore in this competitive world. For instance, the Bible teaches us not to kill. Would one then lay his life down to another who had raised a gun to shoot at him because he would rather inherit the Kingdom of God? To him, that was the wildest belief.

He was resolved. The next day, he would make contacts, he had not been in Lagos all his life for nothing. He knew the joints to locate the type of men he wanted for the job. After all, he would not be involved. He will be paid for the information. That meant money. What a nice way to pick up the naira. Ten percent was the business figure. Ade began having fantasies of what he would do with the money. He would first sponsor Aduke's party, mend fences with some of his girlfriends. Change his car to impress that stubborn Ibo girl Adaobi who would not succumb unless he changed his car. to a 305 or 505 Peugeot.

Ade was in high spirit when he got home. The moment he parked his VW beetle, he whistled in gaily on Jimmy Cliff's tune "you can get it if you really want but you must ...."

"Darling, Darling." There was no response "oho where has this woman gone to?" he said to himself.

"Darling," he called again as he made towards the kitchen.

"Yes," came an answer from the kitchen. "I am coming please." When she came in, she was in oil soiled wrapper and a dirty frock with her baby nestled in her hand. She looked a sorry sight, not something to show for as the wife of what the villages would call 'senior service'.

"Darling you look dirty in that thing you are putting on. Why?"

"Yes, I will change it with that trunk full you bought for me," she snapped at him. "When you go about playing loverboy about the town forgetting you have a family to look after. Sorry o' it is now you see that I am dirty, I don't know you have eyes. You have my sympathies.''

"Oh! come on darling, Don't be a little fool. I have always told you why things were so with me. But right now, things will have to turn for the better. I told you I invested my money somewhere. Is that not so?''

"Yes, you told me and I know the place. In those whores you go about with. Think I don't know! What a nice investment shame on you Mr. Investment. You have no shame. It is a pity.''

Ade immediately left for the bedroom, his wife was right. It was all his fault, but will he pull this job through? That would restore the relationship.

That evening and the subsequent two weeks that followed saw Ade in most of the joints at Noman's land - Ajegunle. He had his ears to the ground. Changing hotels. At the end of the second week, he was rewarded. He was nursing his fourth bottle in the third hotel for the night when a tough looking man dressed in a french suit and a felt hat covering half of his face walked into the hotel. He look around for a vacant seat but there was none. Just as he was about to leave, the man who sat opposite Ade for the past hour without even responding to his greetings or his casual remarks looked up and saw the man leaving.

"Oga Robin-hood,'' he shouted. An instinct told Ade that this man who dressed so well and still had a gangster name must be an 'operator'. The man looked back and walked towards the caller.

"Oh! It is Roggers.'' walking towards Ade's table.

"How is tonight.''

"Boy no show.''

"Who is that sitting with you, a friend or foe?'' Without waiting for the man to say something, Ade jumped up.

"I am a friend, I am Ade of the Express Bank and I can be useful. Can we talk outside?''

The man assessed Ade. Looked at his companion and nodded his head.

"Okay let's go."

Outside, Ade put them on the picture. Every Friday, a large sum of money was deposited in the bank, if a crack gang was found, he was sure to get the approximate figure to be lodged. It will also be advisable to carry out the operation when the bank prepares for cash lodgement to the Central Bank.

"Okay my friend, come back here tomorrow. We shall see the boss, and bring your figures along with you."

The next day, Ade went through all the ledger in the pretext of looking for some figure for the general ledger. He collected the amount lodged on Fridays for the past two months and compared them. They had been following a steady pattern. Eighty to Hundred Thousand.

Before eight that evening, Ade was already seated waiting for the men.

Both men entered an hour later.

"Now old boy, let us get down to biz," said Robin hood who appeared to be the leader.

"Have you the papers, and what is the estimated amount in two weeks from now?"

"I have the papers. In two weeks, I expect between Eighty to a Hundred Thousand naira."

'That is alright'. How is the security there and who is with the key to the safe?"

"There is only a police constable by the door. The key is with the Accountant that sits beside me in the Office."

"Well, see us here two weeks for your cut, but remember, if there is a hitch, your-life will not be worth anything. Also, if the show falls below fifty, no cut for you. Is that clear?

"It is clear."

The normal business in the bank premises was on two weeks later when four men with hats drawn over their faces walked into the bank with brief cases in their hands. They looked like the normal bank customers, even the police constable sitting by the door with his Mark IV rifle resting by his side as he watched the customers going in and coming out did not notice anything unusual about the men and the brief cases they carried.

The only exception to this was Ade who quickly recognized one of the men as soon as they came in. He wanted to alert the accountant, the police, everyone to run for their lives out of fear, but remembering that he needed money badly and also the threat of the gang, he thought better of it. He was sure they must have identified him. He would be the first to be shot if things went wrong. He buried his head in the ledger on his table praying when he heard the first shout and the blast of a gun.

As if by a signal, the four men had flicked open their briefcases simultaneously and from there emerged automatic refles. One took over the entrance covering the police constable and relieving him from his normal duties. The police constable just stared at the nozzle of the automatic. One covered the Manager's Office while one covered the frightened customers. Few shots were fired in the air as a warning to the fear-stricken customers that the guns were no toys but loaded with bullets. The leader of the gang made straight for the accountant's table.

"Hand over the key to the safe," he howled at him. Without hesitation, the accountant opened a drawer and handed over the key. He jabbed his elbow into the man's side and he fell over his seat.

In a split of a second, he had the safe opened. The brief cases were stacked with money. Satisfied, he pushed the safe close. As he was going out, he ran two shots into Ade who had been identified as they came in, by one of the contactment. It was the mafia style, the law "Omerta", the law of silence. Ade fell on the floor writhing in pain.

"Mo ku o! Mo ku o! Iya mi o. Mo ku o!

He ran in more shots to finish him off. With speed like lightning the men sped out. The operation was over.

At the T-junction, near the bank, they ran into the anti-robbery squad patrol car. The patrol car ran after Obi and his men. Obi and his men sensing danger fired at the policemen. A gun battle ensued. Unfortunately for Obi and his men, a bullet got one of their tyres and the car sagged to a stop. Quickly Obi and his men ran out. "Heavy Rain" and "Dan Blocker" gave the rest of the gang a covering fire. Under seconds, Ade was at the steering of a commandered 504 Peugeot. But before they could all enter, Heavy Rain and Dan Blocker received the lead inside them. They were unconscious. Obi glanced back, saw he could not do anything to help them, ran more shots to finish them as the car zoomed off to escape. It was the law of the mob, Omerta, the law of silence. A wounded gangster in the hands of the police was a great threat to the hundred alive.

Terror had been out of action for some two months. The bank raid unnerved him. It nearly made him. His escape was spectacular. It was a deep mystery that he escaped with the bullet wounds. The gunbattle with the anti-crime squad was gruelsome and at the same time explosive. It was under the cover of this fire that Obi made his escape. All in all, he lost two members of his dare-devil gang; "Heavy Rain" is sharp shooter and "Dan Blocker", his next-in-command.

The massive manhunt for Terror was spread all over the states where they thought he might be. But Obi remained immured in his cosy flat at the exclusive Badagry G.R.A. Dr. Ojo was in attendance. He gave in his professional best. Considering the one month deadline given to him, he made a quick job of it. Within a month and half, Obi was up again. The hunt was carried to his doorsteps, but little was achieved. Most people closed their eyes and pretended they knew nothing.

With him was Ade, a member of the gang who served as his cook, washerman, steward, body guard all rolled in one, he was in fact a factotum. They went out only in the evenings under the cover of darkness to his mistresses rotatingly.

Though Obi had over half a dozen women dangling after him, he never considered it a serious affair. No relationship was serious. It was come easy, go easy. He regarded his women as toys. Things to play with and discard. There was no sentimentality over any woman. These women were selected from the cream of the prosperous women who had thrived on his spoils. They saw him as an end to their means. Obi did not live in sex; rather, he saw women as component parts necessary for human existence, a thing that makes life a little bit worthwhile. Money, and good women were all a man needed to keep on, and he had all.

Obi had at the present no consideration for marriage. His job involved great risk. Marriage would mean taking one of his mistresses as a wife, that he would not do. They were not decent for him. They had indulged themselves in too much crime to make good mothers. When he retires from active service, that would be in three or four years, he would find himself a decent girl from any part of the country for procreation.

Most often, Obi knew that the presence of these women irritated him, but they had become part of him. Apart from being members of the gang and sometimes performing professional jobs in collecting vital information from men, they satisfied his insatiable sexual urge. He could lay three women a night all line up and would be ready for a mile race the following morning.

Meanwhile, his fieldmen had been pouring in vital information. The information required analysis. It was from this hideout that Obi got the information that set the ball rolling for the execution of the robbery that hit the headlines and considered the greatest in the annals of crime all the states over. It was this robbery that flushed the police from their cocoons and set them after the No. one enemy, Terror.

Three months to the month of Christmas, Terror was in his hideout with one of his mistresses when one of his fieldmen requested to see him. The man was promptly shown in. He was just turning round in his mind the hot proposals dropped on his lap that afternoon by the Wages Manager of the Continental Supply Company when Terror came in from the connecting door clad in expensive pyjamas. Obi never mixed business with pleasure. Business first and pleasure later. Obi had immediately jumped off his woman when he heard he was being looked for by a field's man. He knew no fieldman dare came to him unless something clicks.

When Obi came in, the fieldman quickly stood up and bowed in reverence.

"Good evening, Sir."

"Good evening Umoru, What is biting you? Sit down. Whisky or beer?"

"Beer, Sir."

"Ade!" he called out." Let us have two-bottles for a start."

"Yes Sir" came the answer from the kitchen.

It was Obi's policy to treat his men fine and as equals when not in operation. That gave them a sense of belonging. Most often, at his leisures, you would hardly come to believe that he was the same hard and stern Obi. He called it good public relationship.

When the beer arrived, they poured into their glasses and cheered.

Obi cleared his throat after a slip.

"How is the field, Umoru? Nothing seems to be coming in towards your angle. It seems you are resting on your oars."

"Sir, not so, we are faced with a host of difficulties. The competition is there, every company is becoming more careful, no loopholes. People are becoming wiser. Nevertheless, I had a tip off this morning."

"Yes, give it to me."

"A man from the wages section, to be precise, the Wages Manager of the Continental Supply Company----"

"What do you say?" Obi cut in. The name opened up fresh wounds in his mind.

"I said the wages manager of the Continental Supply Company gave me a tip off this morning. He said that a total of One Hundred and Fifty Thousand Naira will be paid out in December as salaries, wages, leave grants, overtime and bonus. He is ready to supply more information if promised a fair share and protection.

Obi nodded his head in agreement.

"Continental Supply Company?"

That was the Company he had worked for. The company that had sent him right into jail unjustly. Sudden creep for vengeance rushed into him. Yes, he must carry out his assault to the very company that humiliated him. Here was his opportunity. The Director, everyone in the company must be affected by the cyclone that would blow. They must all bear the brunt of the injustice he suffered some years back five or six years. He had been impelled to crime just for the sake of vengeance and now he was carrying it to the very doorsteps of the Organisation that had been instrumental in its perpetuation. He now had the opportunity to make up for what he suffered.

Umoru saw excitement written on the face of his boss. That made him happy. It was seldom that people impress Obi.

Obi looked up at Umoru.

"What did the Manager call himself?"

"Isaac, Sir, he is an Ibo man."

"Isaac?"

"Yes, Sir."

He remembered that Isaac was a wages clerk while he was the invoice clerk. He wondered how he had warmed himself to that position. His thought dwelt on his relationship with Isaac while he was still there. It was not very cordial. Isaac had a lean look, never smiling. He remembered the only time they had fallen apart because of money Obi lent him which he refused to pay back. Could Isaac be the person who brought all these troubles to him? It disturbed his mind.

Though he had no proof, but intuition told him it was him that was the nature that played on his destiny. He wondered why it did not occur to him then. He now thought of Isaac in this new image. Yes! If he could afford to think of such a large scale 'deal', he must have been responsible for that too. He was going to nail him for it. Find out and if true and would do it personally. First, he would execute the deal, and execute Isaac in the mafia style for his part. This was killing two birds with a stone.

He purred with delight on this deal. Apart from the taking, there was the opportunity to settle an old score.

"Umoru."

"Sir."

"When do you hope to meet the man again?"

"In two days' time."

"Well, I am going to place this responsibility in your hands. You negotiate with him. Agree to any term he suggests, I will like to remain anonymous. I will operate from the background. Obtain all necessary figures and time needed. I will like to see you here after you have seen him. Is that clear?''

"Yes Sir."

Just then, Alhaja Binta peeped from the bedroom annoyed. She had been left in the middle of a sexual act.

"Terror, what do you mean, leaving me like that?''

"Come on get inside and wait for me!'' Obi shouted at her. She obediently withdrew her head. Turning to Umoru.

"Umoru, you are expected here on Friday night for feedback. Is that clear?''

"Yes Sir."

"Okay bye! Wait!'' Obi went to the drawer, opened it and extracted five, twenty Naira notes and handed them over to him.''

"Have this.''

"Thank you, Sir.''

When he left, Obi went back to the bedroom. Alhaja Binta was sprawled on the bed naked. He just dived on her and entered her, pumping ferociously. Alhaja's responses were accompanied with screams. As Ade came in to ask, if Obi was ready for dinner, he heard Alhaja screaming.

'This Oga sef,'' he said to himself and went back to the kitchen. On Friday evening, Obi sat on the lounge chair sipping his beer and waiting expectantly for Umoru to come. He waited till 11:00 p.m. Still no trace of Umoru. He became impatient and edgy. Could it be that Umoru has messed up things? Couldn't he have handled it himself and better? No. If the theory he was working on was true, his presence could have spoilt everything. Isaac could not have trusted him.

The knock at the door startled and irritated him and at the same time sent him jumping up. He rushed to the door and opened it.

"Good evening, Sir.''

"My friend, why did you keep me so long?''

"Sir, the man was trying to be difficult.''

"What do you mean by being difficult?''

"He nearly changed his mind. He also demanded half of the takings.''

"Didn't I tell you to agree on any terms he suggests? Are you a fool?''

"Sir, I could not have done so without some arguments. That could have made him very suspicious."

Obi looked at Umoru. He liked the sense behind the argument. Consenting immediately could actually make somebody smell a skeleton in a cupboard. In his anxiety, he had lost all his wits.

"Well, how does it stand now?"

"Everything is okay, Sir. I promised him Fifty Thousand Naira if the taking is a Hundred and Fifty Thousand and less if the money is less. But I made him realize that we will not do any deal below Fifty Thousand. If it is below it, he gets nothing."

"That is a fine deal. Did he release any leading information that might help?"

"Yes, Sir. He goes on escorted with a police constable. He collects the money from Union Bank in a Toyota Landcruiser."

"Is that all?"

"He said pay day is on Monday. If we need to study the movement to be sure, we can."

"That is alright."

"For his own interest, he wants the operation to take place between the Office and the bank?"

"Does he look like a man who will stand by the deal till it is executed?"

"I feel so, Sir. From the experiences he recounted, he is not a new man in the deal."

"What type of experiences did he recount that makes you believe him?" Obi asked, masking the anxiety mounting in him.

"Sir, at least he told me he had carried out minor operations, but the major ones was the one he did when he was still a wages clerk. I can't remember exactly the date he gave."

"Go on, forget about the date," snapped Obi, he was getting very anxious. His thinking had been right.

"He said a man approach a clerk in his office just for specimen signatures and invoice booklet. But the clerk had no heart to rock the deal. When later the man approached him with the offer, he not only supplied the signatures and the invoice booklet but supplied the clerk's signature. The deal was carried out, Five Thousand for him and three years jail for the clerk," he had chuckled.

"That was quite splendid," Obi said. He hid the anger on his face. "Then he is our man."

"Now you can go. Come and see me tomorrow by this time. I must have completed plans."

"Yes Sir."

"Call me Ade as you leave."

"Yes Sir. Goodnight Sir."

As Umoru left, Obi went to the cabinet and brought out a bottle of whisky and poured himself a glass to steady his nerves. Ade peeped in as he was pouring the drink.

"You called me Sir."

"Yes, give me a very big roll of "GEM." (Marijuana)
"Yes Sir."

When the "gem" arrived, Obi puffed on it. His mind was on the little information he had gathered that evening. His vague ideas has crystallized into the truth. So it was Isaac who sold him out. His three years in jail earned Isaac five thousand naira". His crave for vengeance increased. He must make Isaac confess his crime before his execution. The money didn't mean much to him now but the desire to see Isaac kneel down and beg for his life.

He quickly started to map out the plans for the operation. Isaac would be asked to come that evening at a bus stop where he will be picked up by his men for his own share of the money From there, he would be driven straight to the mobs torture room at the outskirts of Agege. He would be there waiting for him, if he survived the shooting. All these however, depended if he survived the shooting. To guide against this, Obi had given instruction to his men not to shoot the manager. It was his meat. He would deal with him personally. He knew that Umoru must have wondered why he so readily parted with such amount without the execution of the deal. It was unlike him to do so. He knew he did not understand and would never understand. Though late, this information could have saved him from going to jail. It was the absence of the information that made him a criminal, that made him a killer. He could have paid any amount to any other person outside his mob who had brought him this information. It meant a lot to him. He was now thirsty of the blood of the man who made him a bloody man.

That night, the action committee of the gang was summoned. They drew out their strategies based on the information supplied by Umoru. The operation was to involve Obi himself leading, Ade the driver and two other marksmen. A fifth man was to create a go-slow for the target at the action spot. It was agreed that the Company be kept under surveillance especially on pay days.

A spot was selected along the route between the bank and the Company.

That night, Obi slept on the whole plans. He did not want any hitch in the plans. His particular interest lay not on any other thing but on the Wages Manager, Isaac.

Eventually, the Day arrived. It was pay day, a day when little work was done. All the staff of Continental Supply Company were anxiously expecting their salaries to seal off all their Christmas preparations.

As soon as the Landcruiser carrying the Wages Manager and the police escort left the premises, it was immediately followed by a 504 Peugeot bearing a Lagos State Registration number. The driver, had no difficulty in making it out among the others parked in the premises.

Meanwhile, the gang had taken their position, where the action would take place. The passing of the two vehicles on their way to the bank around 10.00 am was indication to the men to get ready for action.

At the bank, the normal transactions between bankers and their customers were on when the two vehicles arrived. The money was duly collected, packed into the trunks and were loaded into the Landcruiser with the police firmly clutching his Mark IV police rifle.

Isaac was looking up and down like a fugitive. His palms were sweating. Cold sweat were beginning to settle on his forehead. He knew what was to happen to the money he now had loaded in the van. He pitied the police escort and the driver who might lose lives in the process. He looked sternly at the policemen. Their eyes met. He quickly carried his face away and went towards the driver. Near the driver, he stopped short as their eyes also met. There seemed to be an aura of hatred and animosity between the two men. He went into the van and sat quietly. He was quite uneasy. Both men noticed it but were unable to decipher the cause.

As the driver carrying the money inserted the key in the ignition, the driver to the Peugeot entered and his car spurted to life. The driver to the Landcruiser left the bank unsuspecting. He did not see anything extraordinary when the 504 Peugeot quickly manoevered its way to the front. It kept a small distance as it joined the flow of traffic.

As it approached the point where the members of the gang lay in ambush, the gap between the two vehicles was reduced. By this time, the van had come directly behind the car. At the exact point, the Peugeot swerved in the middle of the road and quickly applied his brakes. The driver of the van was caught unawares. To avoid a likely collision, he quickly stepped his legs on the brakes. That was the signature tune. Quickly, the gang rushed out of their hiding. The screeching of the tyres and the first round of shots merged together.

The driver made a bold attempt to escape but was caught by bullets that rained on the van. The robbers were now all out from their hiding. Their submachine guns continued puffing its deadly message. Bullets were sprayed like raindrops at the van. The two men who rushed out to mount road blocks stood like effigies clutching their messenger of death. The machine guns spurted bullets aimlessly, some hit over-zealous passersby. It was rock steady.

Tyres screeched, U turns were made at top speed. Vehicles collided with one another. It was a traumatic saga. A tanker fully loaded with Petrol collided with a Landrover and burst into flames. Vehicles coming were caught in the inferno. It was a continuous action. One car lighting the other. Nobody to the rescue. Everyone struggling for his own dear and precious life. The instinct to survive was supreme.

At the climax of the pandemonium, Terror and his men continued their operation. They moved in punctiliously. It was with precision, their guns spurting fire as they move along. The police escort's Mark IV had no answer to the sophisticated weapon carried by Terror and his men. Even if it had, the escort was incapacitated by two things. Firstly, he had only ten rounds of live ammunitions to guard a sum of One Hundred and Fifty Thousand Naira in this wake of serious armed robbery in the country. Besides, he was caught unaware and could do nothing. Even in his sitting position in the car, he had made a bold attempt to fire five rounds of his ammunitions though aimlessly before he fell in line with the bullets from the gang's line of fire and fell face downwards on the seat.

In a flash, Terror was in the van. He saw Isaac unconscious from some bullets received. He jerked him up but the limp figure fell back.

"Take him to the car," he shouted to one of his men.

The man carried the body of Isaac to the car. He could not understand why the boss had to carry an unconscious body to their escape car, why he did not go for the money first. But who was he to question Terror's words.

Quickly, he brought out the three heavy trunks containing the money and they were immediately transferred to their get-away car. Ade was at the wheels and the engine was kept running. All the doors of the car were kept open. They all got in. The car ricocheted on the culvert and bounced back on the road and sped off.

The operation had lasted only twenty-five minutes. Nevertheless, the maelstrom of the operation was scattered like dry leaves in the harmattan. In all, four cars and a tanker were burnt, seven people including the police escort and the driver were left dead while several others were wounded. The scene attracted public sympathy.

Good Samaritans quickly came to the rescue. Some of the seriously injured were rushed to the hospital. Ironically, among the good samaritans was a member of the gang who was there as an observer. It was a policy of the Public Relations Department of the mob to always leave a member near the scene of any crime just to bring feedback. Ola was there, he saw it all and felt it all. He was moved with pity. He was not an action man himself but he felt that this had gone beyond a limit.

An hour later, the anti-crime squad of the police arrived amidst much siren. They set out to take finger prints on the car. The crowd surged forward. Women wept freely at the sight of the dead. The burnt vehicles were removed from the road to restore the flow of traffic. The pressmen soon arrived. Cameras clicked indiscriminately. The photographers had more pictures to take, hideous pictures of atrocities.

That evening, the Commissioner of Police gave a press conference. In it, he vowed to bring to book the men that had perpetuated such enormous atrocity, the massacre of innocent and defenseless citizens. The search might take time, he asserted, but he was sure they would be eventually caught. He appealed to the public for calm and solicited for their cooperation in helping to track down these enemies of the society.

Not only on this men, but a total war on all undesirable elements of the society. He appealed for public vigilance. Any suspected person should be reported immediately to the nearest police station. He lastly expressed his heartfelt sympathy to the families of the dead and particularly to that of the dead cop who had died while on active service.

Many arrests were made. Many innocent people were also arrested. The police spread their tentacles far and wide. With massive support from the public, they knew they will get at the much sought after criminal but that it would take time. Things became difficult when the public refused to cooperate. But in this case, they were ready.

Back at the joint, the key to the trunks was got from Isaac's pocket. When opened and the money counted it was a Hundred and Fifty Thousand Naira for the workers who had laboured. To them, it would be a Black Christmas, their pay had been snatched.

Dr. Ojo was quickly sent for to revive Isaac, who responded to treatment progressively. Save for the bandaged arm, he was fit to go back a week later.

All this time, he had been kept in a small room, with a high window. He only heard the occassional noises from the house. No one visited him except Doctor Ojo and Alison who brought him food.

Isaac felt he was in safe hands. He felt that the mob was a considerate one who took care of their wounded informant. But little did he realize that they were breeding him for death.

By 9.00 p.m. a week after the robbery, Umoru walked into Isaac's room with a brief case. It contained a sum of Fifty Thousand Naira supposedly to be Isaac's share of the money. The brief case was handed over to him to count the money inside it. With shaky hands, he accepted the case and flicked it open. He carefully counted the money. It was Fifty Thousand Naira. He heaved a sigh of satisfaction. He looked up at Umoru and smiled.

"Thank you. I knew you would fulfil your promise."

"It is always good for business."

"Right, when do I leave here? I have plans to see my family for they must be wondering what must have happened to me."

"You are leaving right now if you are set."

"I am set."

"Wait a minute. My boss is very happy with you. He would like to see you and thank you personally. In fact you impressed him a lot. This might also open up a good working relationship."

"That is okay."

Together, with Isaac clutching the briefcase, they left the room. At the entrance, Terror's Mercedes Benz was parked. Both men entered the rear seat. Ade was at the wheel. He did not glance back at the man. He already knew his fate.

Isaac never for once thought about the boss. To hell with any boss. His mind was pre-occupied with the money he had now beside him. What was he to do with the money now that he has got it. First, he must hide it, and report his presence to the police. He would claim he was dumped somewhere and that he could not identify where he was dropped since he was blindfolded. Pictures of luxury conjured up in his mind. He had his mansion. He had not been able to erect a nice building at home. Now is the time, more he would resign his appointment after the heat has cooled off.

He was in this thought when the car pulled outside an isolated building. An instinct warned him of danger. But the security of the money beside him dispelled any fear he had. He was still with this case when he was led into a room through an expensively furnished sitting room.

The room was dim-lit.

"The boss will see you in a minute," Umoru said and left, closing the door behind him.

Five minutes later Terror walked in.

"Good evening."

"I am very happy to have you here tonight. I took particular care so that nothing happened to you during the raid."

"I am very grateful for that."

"I was getting afraid you would back out at the last minute and you know what that meant in this our line of business. But my man gave me an assurance that you were a man of your words and you had pulled similar deals before."

"That is quite right, when I am in, I am in, unless the associates disappoint."

"But have you pulled any before? I mean documentary business - L.P.O., Signatures, you know we call them documentary."

"Oh yes, I pulled one years back. It was with the same company. Just Thirty Thousand Naira."

"Tell me more about it."

"A guy first approached the invoice clerk we had then, for signatures and an invoice booklet. The new guy refused, trying to play a goodman. When the man approached me, I pulled it fast, I even gave him the signature of the clerk. They used his signature. I got the money and he got three years jail term with hard labour, how about that."

Obi gave a twisted grin, he went to the switch and flipped on the overhead fluorescent light. The whole room was flooded with light. His right hand was still thrusted in his trouser pocket. It held a small automatic pistol.

"Can you recognize the invoice clerk?" Obi faced him, his face set in a tight grin.

Recognition dawned on Isaac.

"Obi," he called in utter surprise.

"Yes Isaac, ten years ago, you had your way. You made me suffer for what I did not do. You sent me to jail. You and your family enjoy at my expense. You made me lose my job, my reputation, worse still my mother. She died of heartbreak because I was sentenced. My sister was forced into prostitution just to sustain the family. But now is my turn for revenge."

"Please Obi, you can have this money back and let me go. I don't need it again. I promise I will not say a word about it to anyone. I am sorry for what happened, please forgive me." Isaac knelt down. His face became a mask of fear.

"No Isaac. Vengeance is sweet. I have lived on it ever since I came out of prison. I am not going to change course now. It is too late. You have made a criminal out of me. I have no regrets whatsoever. But you are going to receive your fair share."

He brought out the pistol, Isaac looked at the nozzle. Still pleading for his dear life. Obi shot him through the pleading eyes, next at the chest. Isaac slumped on the ground dead but Obi kept off loading the bullet on him. He went over to the dead body and kicked it. Satisfied, he left the room.

Inspector Mark sat on his table lost in thought. His chin was resting on his left palm. He had a biro pen making a meaningless pattern on the piece of paper on his table. His mind drifted to the scene of the robbery earlier in the day. The scene made his hair stood on end.

Victoria was Dynamite and surely Dynamite is a dangerous stuff to handle. As a Police Officer, she knew best how to handle men and extract information from them. Her beauty is irresistible. Her boss sized her up as she entered his office and felt his lost confidence in his surbordinates return.

"Vicky, there had been strange happenings around us lately. The crime wave has increased. It seems that the public and in fact the chief is fast losing confidence in this department. Unless one does something to rejuvinate their trust on us, we might be shown out of this department, and that is the last thing I expect to happen to me. I better resign before it happens. I have headed this section for twelve years now. Things had not happened so bad as I am experiencing now. The men I relied on had all left for better working conditions elsewhere. Do you blame them? No, I should have left myself if not for the number of years I have put in. Your life is in constant danger by the menace of the armed robbers. You are not adequately armed, at least, to protect yourself. No incentive. I only have an Inspector to show for my thirty-eight years in the police force.''

Inspector Vicky, picked a manila folder on the table and flipped through the pages while still listening to her boss.

"I only have you. As you know the rest are relatively new in this department, I am now relying on you to restore the lost glory of this department. Do you understand?''

"Yes Sir, I understand.''

"We don't seem to have any lead on this man. We have checked on the number of the car, which was the only thing we got from the crowd at the scene. It bore the name of the Chief and in fact his car was packed in the yard with the mechanic working all day to put it back on the road, and that is why he is boiling. His orders are either you crack the case or be cracked. I am sending you out. You have funds at your disposal, spend prudently. All I want is result and fast too.''

"Yes Sir!''

"You can draft as many men as you may need but all I want is result.''

"I understand.''

Victoria Kabaka or Vicky as she was fondly called by friends and foes alike went back to her office. She sat and appraised the situation. Like he said, the situation was hopeless. No lead. She was twenty-eight and had been in the Detective department ever since she turned twenty-two. That was after graduating with a degree in Sociology. She did not know what made her join the Police. She had other and more attractive offers then. Was it the adventurous life of the police force or because his father was an ex-cop, she could not tell.

This case has now been dropped on her lap.

"Crack or be cracked'' the chief had said.

She knew that the only lead could be picked from drinking parlours or hotels. She drew out her plans. Four police constable were to come each evening at an agreed hotel bar to pick her up as a prospective lay. They have to bargain with her for the spending of the night they were to come to her at her signal. Otherwise, they were to tail any car she left in. With any luck, other people would come to her and maybe she might know about the latest gossip on crime. Maybe if she got lucky she could pick on something.

The first week, found Vicky in most of the clubs at Ajegunle. She would buy herself a bottle of beer and a pocket of Benson and Hedges. She will sip the beer through the whole length of period till a constable showed up. Together they would drive off. Nothing happened. Nobody came to her.

Just as she was trying to give up hope and maybe try a more direct approach to solving the case when a drunk approached her late one night.

"Baby I wanna see you outside."

Vicky stood up and walked out with the man outside.

"Baby I wanna lay you, I don't care what it gonna cost me."

"But I am very sorry, I have a deal with my boyfriend. He will be coming to pick me in an hour's time. We have an operation."

Vicky allowed the word operation to hang in the air. She was not quite sure if she was talking to the right person or not but then, nothing bad in trying.

The drunk looked at her and laughed hilariously.

"You go about kicking with men who make small deal. I deal with big stuff baby."

"Man, most of you are nobody, you just make mouthy talk to impress a lady," she said, feigning annoyance.

"I am not a big talker, I am an action man. Follow me home and I will show you."

"Okay, let me finish my beer." Vicky was just playing for time to allow the police constable to arrive. As she sighted the constable, she left what remained of her beer and left, brushing by the constable and whispered as she did so "follow with the car".

The man was dozing when Vicky tapped him gently on the shoulder. Let's go but remember I am coming back here."

"That is okay."

The distance between the house and the club was just ten minutes drive. The traffic had thinned down.

"Baby, what you gonna take?" He asked as she sat on a

settee in the parlour when they got home.

"Beer."

He emerged from the inner room with two bottles of beer. He opened both bottles and handed one to Vicky.

"What deal do you have tonight, and how am I sure you are in the show."

"In the first place, I won't tell you because I don't want a fast one pulled on me. For your second question," Vicky pulled out the pistol she had in her purse. "Do you think I carry this for fun?"

"I like you, and I believe you. We have a bigger deal next week. My boss and the gang will be here tomorrow. To put finishing touches to the plan. In fact you are a God sent, we have been looking for a young girl who understand the show. Now that I have found you, I feel we can even carry out the operation much earlier than planned.

"Man, I don't buy your story. I am not coming out to your place tomorrow. How do I know you are in the game, how do I know you are not planning to hand me over to those lousy people called police. How do I know if your said boss can plan a deal successfully. I don't want to stick out my neck. I operate a clean deal."

"Come on baby don't be a daft, which deal could be more clean than the Continental Supply deal? We pulled it clean and it was big money. At least I got over twenty thousand bread."

"Okay, you have got yourself a deal. Bye for now." Vicky glanced at her wrist watch to hide the excitement on her face.

"My boyfriend would be at the bar now, a bird in the hand is worth two in the bush. I should be checking out. By the way what time would it be tomorrow?"

"Nine o'clock, and remember, when my boss says it is nine, it is going to be nine or you get a black eye. But by the way, are you going now?"

"I have told you I don't lay with women like you. Prove yourself to be a man after that, I will open up, but till then, no way."

"Okay, wait let me drop you off."

"No please I will take a taxi. I don't want my boy friend to be jealous."

Vicky emerged from the room, he waved a taxi, "Supper Club" Constable Alabi eased the Fiat back to the road and followed the taxi.

Vicky came down from the taxi and saw Constable Alabi pulling by. She quickly went towards the car. "Headquarters please," as she entered the car. "Make it fast."

Back at the Headquarters, Vicky picked up the phone.

"Is that Deputy Chief Mark? Please come urgently, something has been uncovered."

Thirty minutes later, the Deputy Chief, Vicky, Inspector Tony from the intelligence were at the table drawing up strategies.

By 2 a.m., they were satisfied with what they had arrived at. Twenty plain clothes men were mobilized. They were to keep the house under surveillance from 7.00 a.m. in the morning to watch the movement of people to the house and to report the number of men who went in but never came out.

About a hundred anti-robbery squadmen in five cars were to come under cloak of darkness. The switch board for the light for that vicinity was to be put off and put on immediately the raid started.

By 7 p.m. men started going in and out of the room. But by 9 by nine p.m. a total of six men were left in the room. At exactly, 9:10, light was restored to the area that had been in darkness, this was the sign awaited for by the squad. They quickly closed up at the house.

The meeting was in full session and Obi questioning about the new girl when the piercing sound of the siren reached them. The men stiffened trying to make out the direction it was passing to. Before they realize that it was for them, it was late. The armed policemen were already on them. Obi and his men opened fire on the alighting police men.

Nevertheless, it was not easy to arrest a gang of crooks. A gun battle ensured. The gang ran short of ammunition. The policemen sealed off the whole place and sent for reinforcement.

Seeing the hopelessness of his situation, two hours later Obi came out from the house, his hands raised above his head in a sign of surrender, smiling in his fashion even in the face of odds. The police bounced on him and handcuffed him. The other members were arrested.

The trial did not take time. Obi confessed to the robbery and earlier crimes. He was found guilty and sentenced to death by firing squad. The sentence was duly endorsed by the appropriate authority.

As Terror and his men jumped out of the Black Maria handcuffed, the crowd surged forward to glimpse at them. They shouted and jeered at them, calling them names. Terror's name rang a bell of terror, a name that epitomized fear for the masses and dreaded by men of the anti-crime squad, a threat to the entire police force.

Instead of remorse and guilt, his face beamed with smile. He waved at the crowd. He looked entirely unruffled. Handcuffed, they were led to the stake backing the beach. A soldier each meticulously tied him and his gang of six to the stake.

Tied, Terror remained unmoved still smiling at the teeming crowd that came in the drizzling rain to watch the execution of yet another gang of the underworld men, men that had caused great agony and fear in the society. The Chaplain came up to the criminals for a last confession, a confession of a soul whose place was already secured at the right hand of "Almighty" Lucifer sitting on his throne in hell. When it came to Terror's turn, the priest looked at the condemned man's face who appeared to be happy even at the instance of execution and shook his head in pity. Looking up from the paper held.

"Obi, be sorry for your sins."

"Needless, Father," Obi replied.

Obi's reply surprised him the more. Obi gave a spasm of laughter. Confession of sins now? That could have been meaningful years ago. Right now, what does it matter to him. Heaven or hell? He knew that every action had a prize tag, but he was past caring. To him, it was an unregretful life. He achieved his inordinate ambition and that sufficed.

Come to think of it, what type of God would be ready to forgive him after all the astrocities he had committed? He thought with the priest still standing in front of him. He could not understand this God, ready to forgive at the zero hour, forgive him who had killed in tens, without inhibitions, robbed people of their properties with impunity, made husbands undress their wives for him and are raped in the presence; made women widows, made children orphans. It was a deep mystery to him. He still did not feel convinced that his sins could be forgiven. His, he thought, had passed the level of being forgiven. His cup had filled to the brim and even overflowed, he sighed.

Before this time, in his ten years of active crime, he never felt remorse. He had not considered himself a sinner. His, was based on a philosophy that "Sin is in the mind." What ever you do and feel you have sinned, then it is a sin. In fact he felt there was nothing like sin, it all depended on the mind. He took to crime for vengeance. Therefore, he had a justification though not morally right.

It was a profession that gave no room for sentimentality; it was a misconduct and unethical to do so.

With the presence of the priest, however, he was shakened, he recalled the Sunday school back home, his mother's piety and untiring effort in trying to make him work in the light of God even in the face of suffering and frustration. He saw the picture of his father carrying a collection bag walking the whole length of the aisle of the church during offerings on most Sundays.

Just then, he heard the echo of the splashing water behind him, it sounded like the voices of the people he had murdered in cold blood seeking vengeance. He shut his eyes as if to erase it off his memory. Then he saw in his closed eyes, the pool of blood of the innocent citizens he had slaughtered flowing towards him in great floods to consume him. He quickly opened his eyes in fear and saw the priest still standing there. He sighed, cold beads of sweat settled on his face. His spirit was in great torment.

"Obi, I say, be sorry for your sins."

"Can God really forgive me?"

"He will if you are sorry for all what you did and ask for his forgiveness."

"Okay father, I am really sorry for my sins and pray for

forgiveness.

"May the almighty God forgive you your sins and grant you eternal rest through the mercy of our Lord Jesus Christ, who live and reign in the Unity of the Holy spirit, one God forever and ever."

"Amen."

As the priest left Terror, a new light shone on his face, new happiness surged into him. He burst into an old favourite Christian spiritual.

The crowd shouted at him in disagreement.

"NO NO!"

"Na lie God no go accept you."

Some wondered what need it was to draft a Chaplain to a firing squad for a last confession. After all these killings, if God would be ready to accept such souls, then their position with God might need reconsideration.

Attention! The voice of the Captain-in-charge of the squad rang out.

There was a mini-parade by the soldiers to get on the mood and in honour of the departing criminals.

By 10:00 am. the volley of shots rang out. It pierced the bodies. Terror's head slumped on his shoulder, his body sagged down.

As the doctor went forward to certify the robbers dead, the crowd began dispersing. Most of them have some questions on their minds.

"Will the execution of robbers bring an end to armed robbery in this country? Won't a campaign against the societal attitude towards material acquisition be more meaningful? Would it not be better to fight the root cause? Rather than execution? Are these people the only enemies of the society? What of the embezzlers of public funds? Who come out and feel no remorse, even spray the naira in the presence of the poor at parties, are their offences not more?"

Nevertheless, at least some were satisfied that this execution had marked the end of a Terror.